小鸟坐禅

XIAONIAO ZUOCHAN

时代出版传媒股份有限公司
安徽文艺出版社

作者简介：

  王长征，诗人、书法家。中国东方文化研究会社会艺术委员会顾问、中国成人教育协会文化创意委员会专家组成员，中国通俗文艺研究会诗歌委员会秘书长，中华五千年动画工程促进会碑拓工作委员会副主任，中非共和国驻华大使馆文化顾问，安徽省当代诗歌研究会副会长，香山智度书院秘书长。文学作品见于《诗刊》《中国作家》《星星》《扬子江诗刊》等文学期刊及百余种选本，出版诗文集多部，被译成英、法、俄、日、韩、泰等多个语种。现居北京，主编《中国汉诗》。

  About the Author: Wang Changzheng is a poet and calligrapher. He serves as a consultant for the Social Art Committee of the China Oriental Culture Research Association, a member of the expert group of the Cultural Creativity Committee of the China Association for Adult Education (CAAE), the secretary-general of the Poetry Committee of the China Popular Literature and Art Research Association, the deputy director of the Monument Rubbing Council of the Committee of Cartoon Project for Promoting Chinese 5000-Year-Old Culture, a cultural advisor of the Embassy of the Central African Republic in China, the vice president of Anhui Contemporary Poetry Research Association, and the secretary-general of Xiangshan Buddhist Philosophy Academy. His literary works have been published in literary journals such as Poetry, Chinese Writers, Stars Poems, Yangtze River Poetry Journal, and over a hundred anthologies. He has published numerous collections of poetry and prose, which have been translated into multiple languages including English, French, Russian, Japanese, Korean and Thai. Currently residing in Beijing, he serves as the chief editor of Chinese Poetry.

小鸟坐禅

Written by Wang Changzheng / 王长征 ◎著

Translated by Chen Shaomei / 陈绍梅 ◎译

XIAONIAO ZUOCHAN

时代出版传媒股份有限公司
安徽文艺出版社

图书在版编目（ＣＩＰ）数据

小鸟坐禅：汉英对照/王长征著．—合肥：安徽文艺出版社，2024.9
 ISBN 978-7-5396-8073-6

Ⅰ．①小… Ⅱ．①王… Ⅲ．①诗集－中国－当代－汉、英 Ⅳ．①I227

中国国家版本馆 CIP 数据核字（2024）第 078456 号

出 版 人：姚　巍
责任编辑：周　丽　　　　　　　　装帧设计：徐　睿

出版发行：安徽文艺出版社　www.awpub.com
地　　址：合肥市翡翠路 1118 号　邮政编码：230071
营 销 部：(0551)63533889
印　　制：安徽新华印刷股份有限公司　(0551)65859551

开本：880×1230　1/32　印张：8.375　字数：150 千字
版次：2024 年 9 月第 1 版
印次：2024 年 9 月第 1 次印刷
定价：69.00 元(精装)

（如发现印装质量问题，影响阅读，请与出版社联系调换）
版权所有，侵权必究

目　录

在以诗参禅中完成自我的觉悟／李云　001
颖淮作家群走出的诗歌才俊／丁友星　027

辑一　会意山水

百丈崖　003

情人瀑　007

秋浦河　011

石壁栈道　013

翠微亭　017

云顶山　021

峭壁上的杜鹃　025

铜铃山的金鱼　029

护城河畔一棵桑葚树　033

杜牧的马　037

李白的酒葫芦　041

行走千里拜谒一片水杉　047

告别水乡　051

断掌　053

丛林四脚蛇　057

螃蟹的挽歌　061

靠岸渔舟　064

水的拥抱　066

山梯　068

深潭　072

一块化石　076

辑二　狂心若歇

在拉萨，仰望苍穹是幸福的　083

布达拉宫的傍晚　085

蓝色的湖　087

夜宿草原　089

草丛里一片羽毛　093

草原，也有陡峭的时刻　097

草原的性格　101

傍晚　105

退隐　109

长调　114

爱情的敖包　118

辽河公园　122

写给孝庄皇后　126

蒙古女子　131

怪柳　135

风沙　139

银杏树　143

芦花飞雪　145

广场　149

辑三　一念回心

晨　153

暴雨　155

叶片上山脉起伏　157

在海滩想念远方　159

视大海为新的目标　161

隐约长号　163

凋谢之花　167

黄昏截句　169
林子的悄悄话　173
一个校园女孩　184
枯木龙吟　187
清醒　191
容器　193
山间诗心　195
小鸟坐禅　199
鸟鸣　203
与石头交谈　206
审视自己　210
这里静悄悄　214
穿过隧道　218

Contents

Achieving Self-consciousness by Meditation through Poetry / Li Yun　011

A Talented Poet Standing out of the Writers Group of Ying and Huai / Ding Youxing　031

Part 1　A Bird in the Wood

The High Cliff　005

The Waterfall of Lovers　009

The Qiupu River　012

The Plank Walkway　015

The Cuiwei Pavilion　019

Yunding Mountain　023

Rhododendrons on the Cliff　027

Goldfish in Tongling Mountain　031

A Mulberry Tree by the Moat　035

The Horse of Du Mu   039

The Gourd of Li Bai   044

Walk Thousands of Miles Visit Metasequoia   049

Farewell to the Water Town   052

A Broken Palm   055

A Lizard in the Jungle   059

An Elegy for the Crab   062

The Fishing Boat   065

The Hug of Water   067

The Ladder   070

The Deep Pool   074

A Fossil   078

Part 2 A Horse in the Prairie

In Lhasa, Looking at the Sky is Happiness   084

The Evening at Potala Palace   086

The Blue Lake   088

A Night on the Prairie   091

A Feather in the Grassland   095

Sharp Side of the Prairie   099

Temper of the Prairie   103

At Sunset   107

Go into Seclusion   111

Long Tunes   116

The Obo of Romance   120

Liaohe Park   124

To Empress Xiaozhuang   129

The Mongolian Girls   133

The Unusual Willow Tree   137

Sand Blown by the Wind   141

The Ginkgo Tree   144

Reed Catkins   147

The Public Square   150

Part 3 A Tree in the Temple

Dawn   154

A Rainstorm   156

Mountains on a Leaf   158

Missing on the Beach   160

Sea as the New Goal   162

Faint Rings of the Trombone   165

The Weathered Flower   168

Sentences in the dusk 171

Whispers of the Jungle 178

A School Girl 185

Dragon Chant in Withered Wood 189

Sobriety 192

The Containers 194

The Poetic Heart 197

A Bird's Meditation 201

The Song of Birds 205

Talk to a Stone 208

Look inside 212

A Quiet Moment 216

Through the Tunnel 220

在以诗参禅中完成自我的觉悟

李 云

青年诗人王长征一直是我关注的国内九〇后诗人中较有特质和诗品的诗人之一。他的诗风追求情感炽热和澄静的对峙冲突所产生的诗内质的突变,在观察日常中又细究其事物发生规律的内在矛盾撞击和消解后的和谐情感表达。日前,他寄我一卷名为《小鸟坐禅》的诗稿,翻阅研读之时,扑面而来的是檀香缕缕,经颂阵阵。我欣喜地发现他在诗写作上又有了新的尝试和探索,其诗有了别于其他九〇后诗人作品的面貌和气质。是的,他步入了以诗参禅、诗禅一味的诗境,在觉悟自性的过程中,让诗歌向"新禅诗体"融入和浸透。正因为他是以佛和儒两大学术为背景,并兼容先锋写作的机变,故而他的诗内涵上更为厚重,形式上更为机灵。

以诗参禅,或写禅诗,古往今来有许多巨匠大师为之，并得到诗禅双修，诗禅两圆满。白居易、周邠是这样，诗佛王维、诗僧寒山亦如此，苏曼殊是这样，周梦蝶、林清玄亦是这样的修行，当然还有梁实秋等。"暂借好诗消永夜，每逢佳处辄参禅。"诗与禅在古代文人和僧者那里是不可或缺的精神必需品。

"诗与禅，或者作诗与参禅的关系，是我国文学史、美学史、艺术史、思想史等中的一个重要问题。"季羡林在《作诗与参禅》中如是说出其重要性。钱锺书也著书论之："了悟以后，禅可不著言说，诗必托诸文字。"均强调诗禅双修的重要性。"以诗参禅"可能是诗人王长征在自己人生与现代诗写作中一个重要的自修。如果是这样，或者从这个角度去赏析他的《小鸟坐禅》，不妨也可以把"小鸟"直接理解为诗人王长征本体，那么再可以推导出小鸟坐禅即诗人王长征自己在参禅。他的参禅当然是为了觉悟，王长征在他的诗集《小鸟坐禅》中给我们清晰地勾画出了这几条觉悟的路线图。以下是我的试析：

一、以山水为参禅对象来求自我的觉悟

在诗集《小鸟坐禅》里,诗人写了二十多首与山水有关的诗,其中有《百丈崖》《峭壁上的杜鹃》《情人瀑》《秋浦河》《云顶山》等等,把山水和山水孕育的万物作为自己诗学具象思考物,从中发现它们生存的根本道理和它们对人类尤其对诗人本体的对应影响和观照反应,从而生出诗情,生发诗意之后的顿悟人生意义,这是诗人所追求的写作根本和生存根本。他在《深潭》一诗中写道:"我以卑微的身份,从这样特殊的视角/看到了大地之眸/对整个世界/充满了主人翁的一瞥。"从"深潭"延伸诗意的"大地之眸",再上升到大地(主人翁)一瞥之"整个世界",这时,他用仰视和俯视互相转变的手法让诗意充盈,并以"卑微"之我的"小",反衬"整个世界"之"大"。在大小之间、俯瞰和仰望之间完成一个诗人的世界观、人生观和宇宙观,也让读者看到他的情怀境界的转变,即"看山是山""看山不是山""看山还是山"三重境界之变。还有他的《叶片上

山脉起伏》,从微小"叶脉"到自己的"掌纹",再到大自然山川的多层空间的推导,找到个体人在自然中的位置和纠缠关系,继而升华到自己要把心灵寄托和交付给山水万物之间的情感和理念的诉求。而这样的情感又是现代人大多沉在心底最深处的情愫追求。他在《山间诗心》中已然表白道:"诗心即佛心/欣然下山去/轻轻唱着浅歌/天上落了一幕清洗荷花透亮的细雨。"他已表露了他的诗观,即诗心即佛心。在山水的面前,他意识到人的卑微和渺小,在《一块化石》中他写道:"我们不过是陆地上的过客/你却知道海洋的诞生。""我们观察、瞻仰/惭愧于人类的渺小与无知/那些属于宇宙文明的秘密/全都凝固在这时光的阴影里。"在歌颂山水之永恒之时,他依旧没有忘记个体人在历史进程中的作用。他在《银杏树》中提醒自己"把一切都忘掉吧/但不要忘记少年出发时/心中那片芳春/野原上直逼人眼的葱绿",不忘初心,方得始终,方为觉悟。塔拉·韦斯特弗说:"你当像鸟飞往你的山。"每个人都有自己的山,王长征是鸟,自然有自己的圣山,他是有佛心的人,有佛心的人写诗,一定会写出世上最悲悯的诗。慧能曾云:"只有人才是有自性的,也就是有佛性的。"佛性与诗性皆归一途。

二、以怀古察今为宗旨来求自我的觉悟

怀古,是从已逝去的事理里认清本质,汲取得失教训,做到前事之鉴,以此规避今日所误;察今,是进一步把握今日之新变化、新问题症结所在,以此解决和处理好问题。当然,诗不是解决具体事物问题的钥匙,它的"无用之用"还是让人们有些觉醒,根本达到觉悟。王长征在怀古方面大多以古代的人物命运和历史事件为诗书写的切入点。他的《写给孝庄皇后》怜悯道:"如果做一个普通的平民/拥有朴素的爱情/生儿育女。"以及对孝庄皇后整个人生的惋惜。在《杜牧的马》一诗中,诗人写下没找到杜牧唐代的那只鞋子,"却找回自己",抒发了对杜牧的雄姿英发人生的羡慕。在《李白的酒葫芦》一诗中拿李白的酒葫芦写出其"将进酒,杯莫停"的酣畅人生和诗人追求自由的志向情怀。他的《草原的性格》分明是写成吉思汗的性格:"直到一个叫成吉思汗的勇士为你

洗头/将草原发丝拧成闪亮的箭/充满寒意/与敌人相争。"幽古思今,对于古人的功过成败,或礼赞颂扬,或批评鞭挞,表现了诗人最根本的知识分子的底线意识,不人云亦云。同时,他这些怀古之诗,又不是一般的对古人的生态记录和白描,而是注入自己的重新认识历史、重新认识古人的新的历史观,他的这些可归纳到"新古典主义诗歌"美学范畴,国内也有不少诗人在这块疆土上开拓,只是王长征走得更远,掘得更深。

　　思今或者说是对当下人与事发展的社会本质的思考,这样的诗,一般会流于口语,流于口水,流于琐屑的情感记录和一般情绪的发泄。王长征对日常生活有着不一般的审视和发现,有着不一般的诗歌呈现。他对"傍晚"有自己的书写:"我在诗歌的草原诵读天空的句子/干净而纯粹的风吹过/绿浪翻滚,陌生而冷酷。"(见《傍晚》)这个"傍晚"是他个人"干净""陌生""冷酷"的"傍晚",三个关键词是他对个人傍晚感受的全部内核。他在《晨》中写出:"想变成一个干净透明的清晨/候在你的睫毛上/只为你夜间苏醒/头脑一片空白时/第一时间受到你的垂青。"由自然景变为心灵景，温馨而充满暖意和爱意，这就是他渴望的——晨。这里的"晨"是他需要的"干净透明"。就连他看"翠微亭"时都感慨道："沉默是我的语言/通过鱼跃写诗。"（见《翠微亭》）这是他的有诗意的日常。他在《穿过隧道》中写道："隧道多么黑暗多么阴凉/石多么坚硬，风多么迅疾。""我看见一棵受苦的树/用密密麻麻扭曲的根，紧紧地抓着仅有的缝隙/好像随时可以把巨石的封锁撕开。"这可能是他对社会局部存在的一种发现和认识。此外，他还从日常取象，让具象生意境，这是成熟诗人的标志，比如他对"钥匙"具象的书写。钥匙是我们生活中不可缺少的生活物件，它的延伸意义是囚禁、封锁和敞开、解放。这个具象被很多人写过，写得最好的莫过于梁小斌的《中国，我的钥匙丢了》。王长征的"钥匙"是"分明看见一把涕泪的钥匙/颤颤悠悠靠近一扇门/在都市的秋风中/迟迟没有打开"（见《隐约长号》）。他让长号之声转型为钥匙，从听觉变为视觉，为我们具体了声音的外象，生动又有美感和亲切感。

三、以对人生目的的审视为本体来觉悟

  写诗的目的无非是发现自己的内心，发现他人的内心，认识自己的精神世界，认识他人思想和世界内部的秘密的过程，审视自己是最根本的，这也是王长征的《小鸟坐禅》的写作根本要义。他用众多的诗来阐释和抒发自己对人生目的和意义的审视和思考，而完成其顿悟。他在《审视自己》一诗中写得很明了："我愿让自己／不断跳出自己。""感受生命的核心本质／卑微与宽广的交替／粒子中的无限世界。"他立志要做一个"不断跳出自己"的人，即舍弃"旧我"，蜕变成"新我"。这种自我否定，自我更生，在扬弃和否定之否定哲学的上升变化过程，化蛹成蝶，涅槃重生，这是一种积极向上的人生态度，是值得倡导的积极人生观念。

  面对厄运或低谷，他用诗作为振奋不屈的人生呐喊，他的诗歌也是人生抗争的檄文。《黄昏截句》中"涛声不倦的古峡／抱住一颗流浪的心／两间茅屋／徐徐从雨后长出"，此时的"两间茅屋"

是流浪者的身体庇难所，更是精神寄托的家园。《鸟鸣》里他用叠词以及具象多变的技法写出了一个生机勃勃的意境："让鸟鸣唤醒树林/结出更多的鸟鸣。""让晨曦更像晨曦。"这里诗人对人生的看法是持着希望和祝愿的态度。他还在诗中不断提醒自己"脚下，万丈深渊""稍一疏忽/便一失足成千古恨"，但他又"无视险境/脚步会更加稳健有力"（见《石壁栈道》），这是他面对厄运降临时谨慎而又坚定向前的人生观，在他的诗行里少有颓废，沮丧的"冷色调"和"灰色调"的情绪流露。在当下诗坛多沉闷愤懑、低落哀愁的诗风里，我们需要王长征这样的阳光、干净，言之有物，扎实的诗。

其实王长征还在以语词提炼术为技能来自我觉悟，这也是他以诗参禅的做法。比如《秋浦河》中"迎春花，这金黄的襻扣/缀在秋浦河细瘦的裙裾"，《视大海为新的目标》中"五指张开，明天向我奔来/五指聚拢，沙漠长出新绿"，《云顶山》中"白云坐遍山丘""于心尖掐出朵朵莲花""把松鼠喊成火焰，把流水唤作歌声"等。这些隽永睿智的语词在多变的组合后，变得有张力，同时也完成了诗人觉悟过程心境图像的再现。炼词炼句是一门以诗参禅过程中必不可少的功课,也是一个诗家写作必修的功课。

王长征在《容器》一诗中写道:"如果写诗是一种修行/日子也可以是一种容器。"祝愿王长征在今后的写作日子里,早日实现自己"以诗参禅"的修行,步入自觉、觉他的大境界。

是为序。

(李云,安徽省作家协会副主席、秘书长,诗人,评论家,编剧,小说家)

Achieving Self-consciousness by Meditation through Poetry

Li Yun

Young poet Wang Changzheng has always been one of the distinctive ones among the post-90s generation poets in China that I have paid attention to. His poetic style pursues the sudden changes in the essence of poetry caused by the confrontation and conflict between passionate and calm emotions, while observing the internal contradictions that occur in daily life and examining the harmonious expression of emotions after collision and resolution. A few days ago, he sent me a poetry anthology *A Bird's Meditation*. Reading it, I was greeted with strands of sandalwood fragrance. I am delighted to find that he has made new attempts and explorations in poetry writing, and his poetry has a unique appearance and temperament that is different from other post-90s poets' works. Yes, he entered a poetic realm of contemplating Zen through poetry, in the process of self-awareness, he integrated and immersed his poetry into "New Zen Poetic Style". Based on the two major academic backgrounds of Buddhism and Confucianism, his poetry has become more profound in connotation and clever in form, compatible with the changes in avant-garde writing.

There have been many great masters throughout history who practice meditation through poetry or write Zen poetry and have achieved both perfection in poetry and Zen. Bai Juyi and Zhou Yao practiced the same way, as did Wang Wei, the Buddhist poet, and Han Shan, the Buddhist monk, Su Manshu, Zhou Mengdie and Lin Qingxuan, and of course, Liang Shiqiu and others. "Borrowing good poetry to dissipate the long night, and frequently meditating in the clever of words." Poetry and meditation were indispensable spiritual necessities for ancient literati and monks.

"The relationship between poetry and Zen, or

between poetry writing and meditation, is an important issue in the history of Chinese literature, aesthetics, art, and thought. " Ji Xianlin stated its importance in his book *Poetry and Zen*. Qian Zhongshu also wrote a book on it: " After enlightenment, Zen cannot be spoken, poetry must rely on various words to express it. " Both of them emphasized the importance of cultivation of poetry and Zen. Using poetry to meditate— maybe it's an important self-cultivation of Wang Changzheng in his own life and modern poetry writing. If this is the case, or to appreciate his *A Bird's Meditation* from this perspective, it can also be directly understood that Wang Changzheng is exactly the Bird, then it can be deduced that A Bird's Meditation is Wang Changzheng' meditation. His meditation is of course for enlightenment, and Wang Changzheng clearly outlined these paths of enlightenment in his poetry anthology *A Bird's Meditation*. My analysis is listed below.

I. Seeking Self-awareness through the Use of Mountains and Rivers as Objects of Meditation

In the poetry anthology *A Bird's Meditation*, the poet wrote nearly twenty poems related to mountains and rivers, including *The High Cliff*, *Rhododendrons on the Cliff*, *The Waterfall of Lovers*, *The Qiupu River*, *Yunding Mountain*, and so on. He regarded mountains and rivers and all things nurtured by them as his own poetic thinking objects, discovering their fundamental principles of survival and their corresponding influence and reactions on humans and even the poet's body, thus generating poetic sentiment, the realization of the meaning of life after the emergence of poetic sentiment is the fundamental factor of his writing and survival. In his poem *The Deep Pool*, he wrote:

Humbly and occasionally from this special viewpoint

I have seen eyes of the earth

to the whole world

gave a master's glance

Extending from the "deep pool" to the poetic image "eyes of the earth", then to the "whole world" it "gave a master's glance", by this, he used the technique of changing perspective up and down to perfecting the poetry, and used "humble" of my "small" to contrast "greatness" of the "whole world". By the changing of perspective and size from small to big, the poet's worldview, values, and cosmic are completed, and also the readers are allowed to see the transformation of his emotional realm, that is, the triple realms of "seeing a mountain as a mountain" to "seeing a mountain as something else" to "seeing a mountain still as a mountain". In his poem *Mountains on a Leaf*, which deduces the multi-level space of nature's mountains and rivers from the tiny "leaf veins" to his own "palm prints", and then finds the individual's position in the nature and the entanglement relationship. It then sublimates to the pursuit of emotions and concepts that he wants to place and deliver his soul to mountains and rivers, which is exactly the deepest pursuit that most modern people hide in their hearts. He has already expressed in his poem *The Mountain Poetic Heart*:

The poetic heart is also the Buddhist heart

Happily, I descend the mountain with a joyful song

A clean rain falls and purifies the lotus flowers

He has already revealed his poetic view, that is, the heart of poetry is the heart of Buddha. In front of the mountains and rivers, he realized the humbleness and insignificance of humans. In *A Fossil*, he wrote:

We are just passersby on the land

but you know the birth of the ocean

We observe and admire you

We are ashamed of humanity's insignificance and ignorance

All the secrets belonging to cosmic civilization

are frozen in the shadow of time

While eulogizing the eternal nature of mountains and rivers, he still did not forget the role of individuals in the historical process. In his poem *The Ginkgo Tree*, he reminded himself:

> Let everything be forgotten
>
> but don't forget the lush spring fields
>
> in the young man's heart
>
> when he sets out

Never forget why you started, and you can accomplish your mission, this is the way to enlightenment. Just like Tara Westover ever said: "You should fly like a bird to your mountain." Everyone has their own mountain, for Wang Changzheng, he is the bird and naturally has his own holy mountain. He is a person with a Buddhist heart, and when he writes poetry, he will surely write the most compassionate poetry in the world. Huineng once said: "only humans have their own nature, that is, only humans ocuppy the nature of Buddha." Both Buddhist and poetic qualities return to the same path.

II. Achieving Self-consciousness by Recalling the Past and Examining the Present

Recalling the past is the process of recognizing the

essence of past events, learning from gains and losses, and thus to avoid mistakes; observing the present is to further grasp the new changes and crux of the new problems today, in order to solve and handle them well. Of course, poetry is not the key to solve specific affairs and problems, and its "useless use" still makes people awaken and fundamentally achieve enlightenment. In terms of recalling history, Wang Changzheng mostly takes the fate of ancient characters and historical events as the starting point for his poetry writing. His poem *To Empress Xiaozhuang* pitifully states :

 If you are an ordinary commoner

 with simple love and values

As well as the regret for the life of Empress Xiaozhuang. In the poem *The Horse of Du Mu*, he wrote that he did not find Du Mu's shoes, but " found himself", expressing his admiration to Du Mu's heroic life. In the poem *The Gourd of Li Bai*, he used Li Bai's gourd to write about his aspirations for freedom of "Cheer up, cheer up! Do not put down your cup". *Temper of the Prairie* clearly depicts the character of

Genghis Khan:

A brave warrior named Genghis Khan washed your hair

and twisted the green hair into shining bows that filled with cold

With them, you defend yourself

Thinking about the past and the present, he praises the achievements or criticizes and whips the failures of the ancients, it represents the consciousness of bottom line and independent thinking of intellectuals. At the same time, his poems are not just ordinary ecological records and sketches of the ancients, but rather infused with his own re-understanding of history and the new historical views of the ancients, these can be summarized in the aesthetic category of "neoclassical poetry", many domestic poets have also explored this territory, but Wang Changzheng has gone further and deeper.

Thinking about the present or rather, reflecting on the social essence of the current development of people and things, such poetry generally flows into oral language, saliva, trivial emotional records, and general emotional expression. However, Wang Changzheng has an extraordinary examination and discovery of daily life, with an extraordinary poetic presentation. He has his own writing on "sunset":

> The words of sky I say in the grassland of poetry
> Pure wind blows through the green waves
> There is something unfamiliar and cold (see *At Sunset*)

This kind of "pure" "unfamiliar" "cold" is his personal feeling and the three keywords are all the core of his personal sunset. He wrote in *Dawn*:

> A clean and transparent dawn I want to be
> waiting on your eyelashes
> If you wake up at night
> with a blank mind
> I will be the first favored by you

Changing from a natural scenery to a spiritual scenery, warm and lovely, which is what he longs for the dawn. The "dawn" here is the "clean and transparent" he needs. Even in *The Cuiwei Pavilion*, he sighed:

> Silence is my language
>
> and by fish's leaps
>
> I write my poetry

This is his poetic daily life. He discovered *in Through the Tunnel*:

> The tunnel is so dark, so cool
>
> The rocks are so hard and the wind is so fast
>
> And
>
> A suffering tree I saw
>
> with twisted roots tightly grasping the only gap
>
> At any time
>
> the blockade of the giant rock could be torn by it

This may be his discovery and understanding of the local existence of society. In addition, he also takes images from daily life to concrete situations, this is a symbol of a mature poet and his concrete writing of the "key". Key is an indispensable living object in our lives, its extended meaning is imprisonment, blockade, and opening up, liberation. This concrete image has been written by many people, and among them the best one is Liang Xiaobin's *China, My Key has Lost*. The "key" of Wang Changzheng is

I saw a tearful key is closing to a door trembling and lingering

But the door had not yet been opened

in the autumn city breeze (see *Faint Rings of the Trombone*)

He transformed the sound of the trombone into a key, transforming it from auditory to visual, giving us a concrete appearance of the sound, vividly yet aesthetically.

III. Achieving Self-consciousness by Examining the Purpose of Life

The purpose of writing poetry is nothing more than to discover one's own heart, discover the hearts of others, understand one's own spiritual world, and understand the thoughts of others and the secrets within the world. Examining oneself is the most fundamental, and this is also the fundamental essence of Wang

Changzheng's writing of *A Bird's Meditation*. He used numerous poems to explain and express his contemplation of the purpose and meaning of life, thus achieving his epiphany. He wrote very clearly in the poem *Look inside* "I am willing to jump out of myself", "To feel the essence of life / the alternation of lowliness and vastness / and an infinite world in the particles". And he is determined to "jump out of myself", that is, to abandon the "old self" and transform into the "new self". This kind of self-negation and self-reliance is a positive and upward attitude towards life and mixes in the process of the rise and change of the negation philosophy, and it is worth advocating as a positive life.

In the face of adversity or depression, he uses poetry as an uplifting and unyielding cry for life, and his poetry is also a testament to life's struggle. In *Sentences in the dusk*:

> The ancient gorge, with its endless waves
> embraces a wandering heart
> two huts
> Slowly grow out of the rain

At this time, the "two huts" are the physical shelter of the homeless and the spiritual home of them. In *The Song of Birds*, he had written a lively artistic conception using overlapping words and the ever-changing techniques of concrete imagery:

Let the song of birds awaken the forest

and produce more songs

Let the morning light purer

Here, the poet holds a hopeful attitude towards life, constantly reminding himself that "Under my feet / the vast abyss is filled with water and rocks" and "Even a slight negligence / can cause a lifelong tragedy", but he also writes "Ignoring danger will make their footsteps more steady and powerful" (see *The Plank Walkway*), which is his cautious and firm outlook on life when misfortune comes. There are few expressions of decadence, frustration, "cold and gray tones" in his poetry. In the current poetry world, which is often filled with depression, anger, and sadness, the poetry world needs more sunny, clean, meaningful, and solid works like Wang Changzheng's.

In fact, Wang Changzheng still uses the technique of extracting words as the skill to realize enlightenment and it is also his practice of using poetry to meditate. Sentences like "Spring jasmine, this golden Chinese knot button ∕ adorns the slender skirt of the Qiupu River" (see *The Qiupu River*). "Opening my palms, the future runs to me ∕ Fingers gathering together, green plants grow out in the desert" (see *Sea as the New Goal*) and "White clouds sit all over the hills and peaks" "pinching out lotus flowers at the tip of their hearts" "calling squirrels into flames ∕ and running water into songs" (see *Yunding Mountain*) and so on. These meaningful and wise words, after changing combinations, become tense and also complete the reproduction of the poet's mental images in the process of enlightenment. Refining words and sentences is an essential skill in the process of meditation through poetry, and it is also a required writing skill for a poet.

Wang Changzheng wrote in his poem *The Containers*: "If writing poetry is also a kind of practice of Buddhism / then the days can also be containers. " I wish Wang Changzheng could achieve his practice of "meditation through poetry" as soon as possible in his future writing, and to step into the realm of self-consciousness and consciousness of others.

The above are my rough insights.

(Li Yun, Vice Chairman, Secretary General of Anhui Writers Association, and also a poet, critic, screenwriter, and novelist)

颖淮作家群走出的诗歌才俊

丁友星

应该说,王长征是我见证成长起来的一位颇具一定影响的青年诗人。十多年前,他还是少年学生的时候,我就发现了他诗歌写作的潜质。他的父亲王瑞也是一位诗人,当时王瑞把他的作品拿来向我请教。仔细一读,我便被王长征创作的溪水般清亮的诗歌深深地吸引住了,内心生出许多喜爱,于是我把这种阅读感受告诉王瑞。从此,我愈加关注他的诗歌成长。如今,十多年过去了,王长征的诗歌已成长为一种有自己个性特征的诗歌,他也因此成为颖淮作家群走出来的一位诗歌才俊。

颖淮作家群乃颖河、淮河流域的一个文学群落。在这个群落里,王长征的诗歌特征鲜明,首先表现出视域宽广。这种宽广,一方面是题材上的,有亲情、友情、爱情,还有社会、自然、哲学,诸如《爱情的敖包》《告别水乡》《百丈崖》《小鸟坐禅》《审视自己》等，似乎为读者展示出他所能打开的一切视域，令人感到他的诗歌涉猎广泛，题材丰富，知识面广。另一方面是地域上的，大江南北，长城内外，无处不在，从《布达拉宫的傍晚》到《草原，也有陡峭的时刻》，从《辽河公园》到《蒙古女子》，从《秋浦河》到《视大海为新的目标》，从《铜铃山的金鱼》到《云顶山》等，王长征的诗歌几乎涵盖了祖国的天南地北、四面八方，令人感到他的诗歌触须已在全方位、多层次地自由伸展，匍匐向前或向上攀缘。

首先，王长征的诗歌表现出精神意味的深层化。诗歌是一门审美要求极高的艺术，因此，它对艺术的审美往往比其他门类艺术的要求更高，在艺术的精神意味上更是如此。正如德国现象学、美学家莫里茨·盖格尔在他的《艺术的意味》里所讲的那样，艺术效果在精神意味上大不相同。一种艺术效果是"艺术对深层自我施加的影响，是艺术的深层效果"；另一种艺术效果则是"艺术对表层自我所施加的影响，它是纯粹的快乐效果或者纯粹的激动效果"。王长征的诗歌似乎在努力追求这种艺术效果的深层化，试图以深层次的艺术效果来引起读者的审美兴趣。例如，在《退隐》中，他通过对草原上"六匹骏马慢悠悠地吃草/眸子呈黑褐色/隐隐还有铁与火的痕迹"施加艺术影响，达到了对这里曾经有过战争深层次的表达。再如，在《清醒》中，他通过对"面包面对着火烤/终于明白/它再也不是/一枝沉思的麦穗"施加艺术影响，同样达到对面包深层次的表达，进而放弃了对表层艺术效果的流连忘返。

再次，其诗歌所表现出思想情感的专注性。这里所指的专注性既有内在的专注性，也有外在的专注性。内在的专注性主要表现在思想意识的内敛，即理性上；外在的专注性主要表现在情感的宣泄，即感性上。若将二者完全统一到同一件艺术作品中，对于一般的艺术爱好者来说，具有一定的挑战性。王长征似乎有种不畏艰险、迎难而上的精神，用他深邃的思想和新奇的诗歌语言接受了这种挑战。例如，在《审视自己》中，他既可以"坐在草地上冥想/陷入空虚的漂浮中"，并且"看到一个赤足的小人/干净纯洁的身体/蹚过汹涌的潮水/静下来，褪去衣服与容貌/静下来，褪去名利和欲望/像柔软的草地接纳星辰日月/在一朵花开放的细节中/剥开层层外壳/深入无穷的细微",也可以"让自己/不断跳出自己/在空荡的宇宙中感受呼吸的强劲/感受一团火的神圣",而且还能感受到"一束光的恒久/感受生命的核心本质/卑微与宽广的交替/粒子中的无限世界"。说到底,这一切都是其思想情感专注性的体现,也是一种不脱离理性主义的感性表现,更是一种不脱离感性主义的理性表达。

王长征还很年轻,未来之路很漫长,因此需要扬长避短,中流击水,更加刻苦修炼。出于欣赏和偏爱,我会一如既往关注他的诗歌创作,期望他能创作出更多、更好、更具豪迈磅礴审美力量的诗歌。

是为序,算是对《小鸟坐禅》这部诗集一种以偏概全的阅读导引吧!

(丁友星,中国文艺评论家协会会员、安徽省阜阳市作家协会主席)

A Talented Poet Standing out of the Writers Group of Ying and Huai

Ding Youxing

Among the young poets I know, Wang Changzheng should be the most influential one. More than ten years ago, when he was still a young student, I discovered his potential in poetry writing. His father Wang Rui was also a poet, and he asked me for advice on his son's works at that time. Upon careful reading, I was deeply attracted by the clear-styled poetry created by Wang Changzheng. Therefore, I shared this feeling of reading with his father Wang Rui. From then on and till this day, more and more attention of mine has been paid to the growth of his poetry. Now, more than a decade has passed, Wang Changzheng's poetry has gotten stronger with its own unique characteristics, making him a talented poet among the Writers Group of Ying and Huai.

The Writers Group of Ying and Huai is a literary community located in the basins of Ying River and Huai River. In this community, Wang Changzheng's poetry has distinct characteristics. Firstly, it shows a broad perspective, which is not only related to its subject matter which includes family, friendship, and love, also aspects of social, natural, philosophical, and religious, such as *The Obo of Romance*, *Farewell to the Water Town*, *The High Cliff*, *A Bird's Meditation*, *Look inside*, etc., seem to show readers all the perspectives he can open up, showing that his poetry covers a wide range of topics, rich themes, and broad knowledge. On the other hand, in terms of geography, from the north to the south, both inside and outside the motherland, Wang Changzheng's poetry is ubiquitous. From *The Evening at Potala Palace* to *Sharp Side of the Prairie*, from *Liaohe Park* to *The Mongolian Girls on Horseback*, from *The Qiupu River* to *Sea as the New Goal*, from *Goldfish in Tongling Mountain* to *Yunding Mountain*, etc., it is felt that his poetic tentacles have freely extended in all directions and at multiple levels, crawling forward or climbing upwards.

Firstly, Wang Changzheng's poetry expresses a profound spiritual meaning. Poetry is an art with extremely higher aesthetic requirements than other types of art, especially in terms of the spiritual meaning of art. As German phenomenologist and aesthetician Moritz Geiger said in his book *The Significance of Art*, artistic effects are vastly different in terms of spiritual meaning. An artistic effect is "the influence that art exerts on the deep-self, and it is the deep effect of art"; another type of artistic effect is "the influence that art exerts on the superficial-self, which is a purely joyful effect or a purely thrilling effect". Wang Changzheng's poetry seems to be striving for a deeper level of artistic effect, attempting to attract readers' aesthetic interest with a deeper level of artistic effect. For example, in *Go into Seclusion*, he exerted artistic influence on the grassland by portraying "six horses slowly graze / with dark brown eyes which are colored by faint traces of iron and fire", achieving a profound expression of the war that once existed here. In another example *Sobriety*, he exerted artistic influence through "Facing the fire / the dough finally understands that/no longer a contemplative wheat ear it is", achieving a deep expression of the bread, and then abandoning the lingering on superficial artistic effects.

Secondly, his poetry expresses a focus on thoughts and emotions. The focus referred includes both internal and external. The internal focus is mainly manifested in the introversion of ideological consciousness, that is, rationality; external focus is mainly manifested in emotional release, that is, in terms of sensibility. If the two are completely unified into the same artwork, it poses a certain challenge for the general art enthusiasts. Wang Changzheng seems to have a spirit of fearlessness and courage to face difficulties, and has accepted this challenge with his profound thoughtsand novel poetic language. For example, in *Look inside*, he can both "Sitting on the grass, meditating/I fall into an empty state", and "A barefooted little person/with a clean and pure body/is wading through the surging tide/Calm down, shedding off clothes and appearance/Calm down, shedding off fame, fortune and desire/Like the soft grassland embraces all the stars/and the details bloom in a flower/I have to open layers of shells and delve into infinite details in my mind", he can also "jump out of myself/to feel the strong breathing in the empty universe/the holiness of a fire", and feel "the eternity of a beam of light/the essence of life/the alternation of lowliness and vastness/and an infinite world in the particles". Ultimately, all of these is a manifestation of his ideological and emotional focus, as well as an emotional expression that hasn't detached from rationalism, and more importantly, a rational expression that hasn't detached from emotionalism.

Wang Changzheng is still very young and has a long way to go in the future. Therefore, he needs to make use of his strengths and practice more diligently in poetry writing. Out of appreciation and preference, I will continue to pay attention to his poetry creation as always, hoping that he can create more poetry with the most magnificent aesthetic power. Above is the preface, which can be considered as a comprehensive reading guide to his poetry anthology *A Bird's Meditation*!

(Ding Youxing, member of China Literary and Art Critics Association and chairman of Fuyang Writers Association of Anhui Province)

辑一　会意山水

Part 1
A Bird in the Wood

百 丈 崖

丽日阳光像个内向的小伙
蹑手蹑脚,在石上重复叠加
一段搁浅的时光
一位赶路疲惫歇息的巨人
安静,站立
等待攀登者造访

百丈是怎样一个距离
你常常望着半途而返的人们
一次次发出
落叶般的叹息

这里不是危崖,亦非险峰
你能感到石头与山峰平等
浅潭与龙池平等

悬崖与幽谷平等
一枚松针，一只蚂蚁
都能受到应有的尊重

百丈崖前
我愿褪去小小的虚荣
做瀑布里的一粒沙砾
书写一个不甚陡峭的崖壁
斜挂云端的理想

The High Cliff

Tiptoed, sunshine is an introverted lad

overlapping and overlapping on the stone

The forgotten time of gold

A weary giant is the cliff

standing quietly

He's waiting for the climbers

He knows well about height

So, every time he sighs

He sigh for the climbers' retreat

It's neither a killing cliff nor a peak

Equality between stones and peaks can be felt

The Shallow Pool and the Dragon's Pool, Cliffs and valleys are all equal

Whether a pine needle or an ant in it

deserves respect of the same amount

Facing the cliff

I wish I can shed off my vanity

and be a grain of sand in its waterfall

to paint the great ideal of the cliff

情 人 瀑

像时光的两行泪水
在忧伤湮灭的时候
仍是情人的两条手链
腰身细腻,缠绕过无数才子佳人的惆怅
一滴水,就足以打湿君王的面颊
痴男怨女
为她掏出千疮百孔的心

来自生命中心的山泉
以敏锐细腻的私语
从高处跌落
于低处汇聚
有着闪电般发光的灵魂
照亮内心最深处的浓荫

在出发地
两棵树相拥相抱
落下来
两条鱼儿吻出亲密水花
被时光抛弃的荒凉
孤零零的我
独自悄然走过

The Waterfall of Lovers

Like two lines of tears of time

She becomes two bracelets of lovers

when sorrow disappears

Her waist is so delicate that the melancholy of countless

lovebirds has been wrapped around

A drop of water is enough to moisten a king's cheeks

For her, the infatuated men and women have dug out

hearts with wounds and holes

The waterfall, originated from the center of life

falls from high to low, gathering

with a sharp and delicate whisper

and a soul that shines like lightning

illuminate the deepest shade of the heart

From the origin

two trees hug together

Falling down

two fish kiss with a water spray

I have been abandoned by time

Alone

I pass by

秋 浦 河

迎春花,这金黄的襻扣
缀在秋浦河细瘦的裙裾
流水远逝
带走王朝兴衰与金戈铁马
属于诗歌的清晨
依然绚丽
以柔情抚慰光阴

柳丝轻扬
波心一点
钓出一位青衫飘逸的书生
在词语的光芒中
擦亮古老的昨天
黎明在手中传递
将一千年来的每一个傍晚
叠成令我心儿微颤的一瞬

The Qiupu River

Spring jasmine, this golden Chinese knot button
adorns the slender skirt of the Qiupu River
The flowing water carries away the rise and fall of dynasties
The beautiful morning belongs to poetry
With tenderness, it comforts the time

Willow branches sway gently
In the center of the river
appears a graceful scholar with a blue shirt
In the light of words, yesterday shines
With the passing of dawn in my hands
every dust in the past one thousand years
folds into a moment that makes me tremble

石壁栈道

每一级台阶都承载着

鸟儿的幻想和天空的托付

扶着蓬勃向上的力

便有了攀登的勇气

比榆钱还小的青苔

翘首远方焚烧过已成黑绿色陡峭的深涧

挥手之间

恐慌与怯懦一圈圈缩小

脚下，万丈深渊

水漫岩石，打磨多少光阴

才形成这光滑溜壁和斑驳的风口

稍一疏忽

便一失足成千古恨

想起被困难层层包裹的岛屿

怎么也迈不开沉重的脚步
青春因风的猛烈而骤然憔悴

是谁在这绝壁之上
开辟一条通途
仿佛一种启喻
血液里蛰伏的火种再次烈焰升腾

常人善以坦途作伴侣
英雄却把天路当成情人
无视险境
脚步会更加稳健有力

The Plank Walkway

Every step carries the fantasies of birds

and the trust of the sky

With the help of the vigorous upward force

one has the courage to climb

The moss, smaller than an elm seed

Watches deep stream afar which has burned into dark

green

In a moment

panic and cowardice shrink

Under my feet

the vast abyss is filled with water and rocks

How many years have passed

before polishing it into such a smooth and mottled

wind gap

Even a slight negligence
can cause a lifelong tragedy
Remembering the islands enveloped in difficulties
I can't take my heavy steps
and my youth suddenly withers due to the fierce wind

Who opened up a path
above this cliff
As if an enlightenment
dormant flame in the blood rose again

Ordinary people takes smooth paths as companions
but heroes treat plank walkways as lovers
Ignoring danger will make their footsteps more steady
and powerful

翠 微 亭

春日寻芳上翠微
田野从四面八方拢来
我听见河水悲壮的哭泣
这是为英雄的遗憾所悲戚
两岸缤纷的花褪去颜色
遥远而陌生
将军和诗人早已远逝
留下惆怅与酒
品味这庄严而隐秘的孤独

面对好山好水
如何为大地而歌
沉默是我的语言
通过鱼跃写诗
眼前是泛黄的历史

身后是喧嚣的尘世
我像个渴望母爱的孩子
紧紧依偎在寂静河湾的臂膊

The Cuiwei Pavilion

On a spring day

I came to the Cuiwei pavilion in the search of flowers

the verdant fields come from all directions

I hear the solemn and stirring cry of the river

a pity for heroes

The colorful flowers on both sides fade away

generals and poets have long passed away

leaving behind melancholy and wine

to taste this solemn and hidden loneliness

Facing the beautiful mountains and waters

how can I sing for the earth

Silence is my language

and by fish's leaps

I write my poetry

There is a yellowed history in front of me
Behind me, there is the hustle and bustle of the world
Like a child longing for maternal love
I tightly nestling in the arms of a silent river

云 顶 山

白云坐遍山丘

山峰硕大的脑袋低垂

秋风奔跑在油画般的绿叶间

大自然赐我沁心的诗句

让温暖的小木屋在浓密的雾中呼吸

俊鸟于窗台上

高一声低一声啁啾

于心尖掐出朵朵莲花

佛光照彻天空

大地披上金色的斗篷

案上的杯中

绿芽伸展慵懒的四肢

浅吟低唱,与天籁应和

房子周围的花朵渐次醒来

俏脸上闪耀浓重色彩
幽香催醒了酣睡的万物
簇拥着每一粒飘浮的微尘

眼睛明亮
耳朵歌唱
生命涌动的四季在蓝天下兴致勃勃
为充满动感的景色命名
把松鼠喊成火焰
把流水唤作歌声

Yunding Mountain

White clouds sit all over the hills and peaks
with their huge heads drooping
The autumn wind running amidst the green leaves
Nature gives me fresh poems
that make the warm cabin breathe in the dense fog
Beautiful birds chirp high and low on the windowsill
pinching out lotus flowers at the tip of their hearts

The light of Buddha shines through the sky
covering the earth with a golden cloak
A cup on the table is filled with green buds
Their lazy limbs stretch out
singing softly in response to the sounds of nature
The flowers around the house gradually wake up
and their beautiful faces sparkle with multiple colors

Fragrance wakes up the sleeping creatures and surrounds every floating dust in the air

Eyes bright, ears singing
seasons are endowed with meaning by creatures under the blue sky
I named for the dynamic scenery
calling squirrels into flames
and running water into songs

峭壁上的杜鹃

特立独行的山间隐士
选择离群索居的生活
可以吮吸充足的空气
沐浴皎洁溶溶的月光
抛却俗世裹缠
眼睛愈加明亮
夜间与山顶的星星对视

光秃秃的一片峭壁
无人打扰
也无人分享风的幽深
选择孤独
不是为了
做不畏艰苦被世人称颂的英雄
因为所处位置

极宜修行
更能坦诚揭开
生与死的秘密
在不断审视内心的过程中
灵魂渐渐通透
感受到宇宙能量的流动

我羡慕你的那份庄严
日月的更替变幻
只是你心尖的一滴清露

什么样的星空
拓出无边的辽阔
九华天池的瀑布
每晚将为你守候

敛去风流才气
在溪水中寻找前世的音容
脱下名利裙裳
彻彻底底做个山野村夫
心底空空
空、空、空——
空

Rhododendrons on the Cliff

The solitary hermit chooses to live a secluded life

in which it can suck in sufficient air

and bathe in the bright moonlight

And in such a life it can abandon the worldly entangle-

ment

to brighten its eyes

And with those clear eyes

it admire the stars on the mountaintop

No one disturbs the barren cliff

Also, no one shares the depth of the wind with it

Choosing to be solitude is not about being a hero praised

by the world

for its daring to bear any hardship

It is because of the perfect position for cultivation

In here, to reveal the secrets of life and death is easier
As the rhododendrons constantly examine their hearts
their souls gradually feel the flow of cosmic energy

I envy the solemn they could have
Alternation of the sun and moon is just
a drop of clear dew on their heart

What kind of starry sky
carves out boundless space
Waterfalls in the Jiuhua Mountain wait for you every night

Shed off the romance and rebels
for the searching of the sound and appearance of the past life in the stream
I am willing to take off the gown of fame and fortune
I am willing to be a village man
with an empty and empty heart

铜铃山的金鱼

碧水清波下的嶙峋怪石
阳光下翻动黑色的脊背
守护大山的金色神灵
水底舞动闪闪发光的鳍

饮水、觅食
音符般游弋在透明的水中
如同摇曳在丛林间的花朵
有时感到它们的鳞片嵌入心间
每当我想交谈
就化作一汪净水

铜铃山经风一吹
发出悦耳的声音
这些静止已久的金鱼

活过一生,抑或永生
它们从神灵的瞌睡中偷渡人间
享受着深山的寂静

面对山间无数棵盯着我的树
我更愿与一条鱼儿对视
它是那样恬静
让我变成一片叶吧
翠绿在这了无烦扰的山间

Goldfish in Tongling Mountain

Like rugged rocks under the clear waves
the goldfish flip their black backs in the sunlight
They are golden deities of the mountain
dancing with sparkling fins

Drinking and foraging
they are notes swimming in the lucent water
and flowers swaying in the jungle
Sometimes I feel their scales embedded in my heart
but when I mean to talk
they dissolve in the pure water

When the wind blows
Tongling Mountain makes a pleasant sound
These static goldfish sneak into the mortal world

lived for a lifetime or forever

from the slumber of gods

to enjoy the silence of Tongling Mountain

Stared by countless trees in the mountain

I would rather gaze at a fish

which is peaceful enough

Let me be a leaf

enjoying the green life in the undisturbed mountain

护城河畔一棵桑葚树

饱吸晨光的果实
在玫瑰色黎明的抚摸下
叫喊着,任由雀鸟的爪子
收拢枝条成熟的诗句

日子平淡如水,略显空虚
甜蜜蜜的黑宝石被遗忘在荒滩
裸露的土地布满腐烂的欲望
它是那样的孤独
颤悠悠压弯的手掌
在绿裙子上羞涩地搓着
在一天天
无人问津的等待中干瘪

在我的村庄

每到夏日,桑葚树上的音符
吸引孩童片片欢呼
它总是带着炫耀和自豪的神情
拥有泥土芳香的白天
和明亮闪烁的白云般的幸福

在护城河畔
这乡村古老的遗民
与超市鲜香的进口水果相比
像一抹空洞的点缀
有些无所适从,有些落寞
多像乡下进城的姥姥
她带来的手捏泥塑
被孩子丢弃在杂物间里
显得那样的萧索、落寞

A Mulberry Tree by the Moat

Under the touch of the rose-colored dawn

the fruit that sucks in the morning light cries

letting the bird's paws gather the ripen branches of verses

The days are as plain as water

with a hint of emptiness and sweetness

The black gemstone is forgotten in the wasteland with

decaying desires

It is so lonely

Its trembling and bent palms

are shyly rubbing on the green skirt

Day by day

it gradually withers in the loneliness

Every summer in my village

the notes on the mulberry trees

attract tons of children's cheers

It always carries a flaunting and proud expression

and a living space that enjoying to the happiness with

fragrant soil and shining white cloud

Compared to the imported fruits in the supermarket

the adherents of village's history by the moat

are like empty embellishments

with loss and loneliness

Just like my grandmother

who enters the city from the countryside

The handmade clay sculptures brought by her

were abandoned in the clutter room by the young

So desolate

杜牧的马

循着诗人残存的足迹

春光一块接一块铺至脚下

在一片踏碎的青石上

捡到杜牧踩出的马蹄

每一瓣月牙印着一首史诗

一滴无所适从的泪

藏着淅淅沥沥的诗魂

清明园

这个硕大无比的春天的器皿

历史在这里

化成细埃微尘

唯有杏花

日复一日地等待

春风送来不胜娇羞的新娘

细数着横笛吹皱的道道涟漪
金黄的油菜花
涂亮忧郁的眼睛
愁肠百结的心绪
被一场突如其来的风雨梳洗
在这里,我没有找到
诗人丢失在唐代的那只鞋子
却找回自己
如识途老马衔回一根竹杖
渐渐寂静下来
是欢悦不眠的时光

The Horse of Du Mu

Following the poet's remaining footsteps

spring spread its color to my feet

On a piece of crushed stone

I pick up the hooves of Du Mu's horse

Each little moon is imprinted as an epic

A drop of helpless tear which hides his poetic soul

Qingming Garden

the vast and unparalleled vessel of spring

has turned history

into fine dust here

Only apricot flowers

are waiting day after day

for its shy bride brought by the spring breeze

With the ripples of the flute

the golden rapeseed flowers

lighten my melancholic eyes

My sorrowful thoughts are also washed away

by the sudden storm

I have not found the poet's shoe which was

lost in the Tang Dynasty

but I have found myself

just like an old horse picked up a bamboo stick

In silence, I encounter a joyful and sleepless time

李白的酒葫芦

世人皆知李白爱酒
却不知他的酒葫芦
掉进秋浦河的波涛
因此,这里每一朵浪花
都洋溢着诱人的酒香

来到池州
走过李白醉卧的岸
不酩酊大醉一回
算不上真正来过

我不担心这里的诗人是否热情
就怕这蜿蜒数十公里流淌的酒
我一个人喝不下
因为她,天空流光溢彩

城市也日益丰盈

万种植物和勤劳的人们

沉浸在爱的汪洋

酒香四溢盈满心房

众水远方浪游

伸出年轻的手轻抚白云

将天空擦拭得瓦蓝瓦蓝

李白丢失的酒葫芦

启喻一种冲入云霄的放荡不羁

饮过秋浦河水

女子愈加眉清目秀

脸上潮出杏花的颜酡

汉子则恨不得骑着宝马良驹

飞驰到唐朝宫殿

钦点贵妃

来一曲《霓裳羽衣舞》

就这样

河以酒的质感名传千古

酒以诗心风流天下

当你来此走上一遭
定能听到河底汩汩喷涌的酒泉
让龙王发出沉醉千年的
粗犷有力的鼾声

The Gourd of Li Bai

Everyone knows that Li Bai loves alcohol

But few knows that

His gourd once fell into the Qiupu River

Every wave here is filled

With a tempting aroma of alcohol for that

Passing by Chizhou's Qiupu River

where Li Bai got drunk

I decide to drink like him

If not getting drunk

then it is not a meaningful visit

There's no need to worry about the enthusiasm of the poets here

I'm just afraid of the alcohol that winds for dozens of

kilometers

can't be finished by myself

With Qiupu River

the sky is shining brightly

and the city is becoming increasingly prosperous

Thousands of plants and hardworking people

are immersed in the river of love

The fragrance of alcohol overflows to the hearts

Wandering in the distance

streams reach out young hands to gently caress the white

clouds

and wipe the sky into blue

The lost gourd of Li Bai symbolizes a kind of unrestrained freedom that has rushed into the clouds

After drinking water in Qiupu River

women's faces become apricot blossoms

men can't help but ride a ferghana horse to the Tang

Dynasty to encounter their own Yang Yuhuan①
who is good at dancing with *Song of Rainbow Skirt and Coat of Feather*②

In this way, the river is famous for its alcohol
and the alcohol flows through the world with a poetic heart
When you come here
with the gurgling and gushing springs of alcohol
you will surely hear the Dragon King's drunk snores
which had flowed for thousands of years

---

① Yang Yuhuan, born in the Tang Dynasty of China, was skilled in singing and dancing. She was one of the famous beauties of ancient China.

② *Song of Rainbow Skirt and Coat of Feather* is a famous court music of the Tang Dynasty. Emperor Xuanzong's favored concubine Yang Yuhuan is famous for her skillful dance of this song.

行走千里拜谒一片水杉

一叶轻舟
回溯于窄窄的水流
鱼跃低于木桨
水鸟收紧翅膀
细碎的阳光斜斜劈开疏影
棵棵水杉站立成俊男靓女
乳白色的水雾中交换着爱情
这人间仙境
虚实间经营着迷人的神话
虾蟹在狭长的水镜中悠闲自在
虫鸣被耳朵摁住
轻吟着十月赞歌

双橹划开水面
人间变得清晰起来

水草曳动着笔直、修长的舞姿
童话里走出的暗影
一次次跌落涟漪
被鸬鹚的翅膀拢进睡眠
树上一声微叹
让思想变成一片轻轻的鸟羽
被水花盈笑着亲吻

哦,水杉
行走千里激情澎湃而来
只为见你一面
当我与你相对而立
不觉间换成了最温柔的目光

Walk Thousands of Miles Visit Metasequoia

A light boat traces its way back to the narrow water flow

Fish dances with the wooden oars

Waterflowls tighten their wings

and the fine sunlight splits through the thin shadows

Each sequoia stands there

like young men and women

exchanging love in the milky mist

This fairyland is filled with enchanting myths

Shrimps and crabs are leisurely swimming in the water

The chirping of insects is suppressed by the ears

Soft hymns in October can be heard

Rowing paddles cut open the water

the human world thus becomes clear

The water grass is swaying with its straight and slender dancing posture
Coming out of fairy tales, shadows fall into the ripples again and again
and are finally taken into sleep by the wings of cormorants
A slight sigh in the tree
turns my mind into a gentle bird feather
which is kissed by the smiling waves

Oh, the metasequoia
I walked thousands of miles to see you once
When I stood opposite you
you can see my gentlest gaze

告别水乡

背靠岩石的小树
根须每天被湖水滋润
纤细的嘴唇
尽情啜饮汩汩清泉

日日夜夜,都在重复着光阴
像勤劳的村民繁衍生息
告别时,我频频回首
没有一片景色肯说"留步"
一首伤感的诗在心中消亡
唯有风,在静静歌唱

Farewell to the Water Town

The roots of the small tree leaning against the rock
are moistened by the lake water every day
and its delicate lips enjoy sipping the clear spring

Day and night, the time is repeated
just like the reproduction of hardworking villagers
As I bid farewell, I look back once and another
hear no "stay" from the scenery
A sad poem fades away in my heart
only the wind sings quietly

断　　掌

木板铺就的栈桥上
一只枯瘦修长的断掌伏卧
像沉睡已久的浪人

它曾与某只水鸟是一个整体
跃上高枝，挑逗白云
沐浴过高空的壮丽景色

如今，静静地躺着
与一条鱼的骨骸相伴
似在诉说一个悲剧故事
几只蚂蚁匆匆赶来
在生命与死亡的纠缠中
水面静如从前
抚摸着周身一切

而岸边,浓荫依然繁茂

藏着串串悦耳的鸟鸣

A Broken Palm

On the wooden bridge

a thin and slender broken palm lies

like a long-sleeping wanderer

Once, it was a part of a water bird

jumping onto a high branch, teasing white clouds and

bathing in the magnificent scenery of the high altitude

Now, lying quietly with the bones of a fish, it seems to

be telling a tragic story

A few ants come in a rush

With the entanglement of life and death

the water is as still as before

caressing everything around

On the shore, strings of birds' song are playing in the lush shade of trees

丛林四脚蛇

慵懒的茶树
绿色的手掌自成一片
山雾弥漫,毛茸茸的掌心向下压着

枯叶在林下沉睡
我安静地走着
孤零零,急匆匆
惊慌失措的小兽疾奔
一朵蓝色火苗从枯黄的布景中撤离

闪电遗落的孩子
整座大山从它腹部穿过

这坠落人间的火焰
色彩斑斓恰似从梦境走出

在我脚边燃烧、尖叫
还有恐慌，天真的眼睛与我对视
紫色的瞳孔宛若蜂蛰
惊魂一瞥，流下细小的泪
我想继续凝神观看
它抖落一棵稻草
带着惊悸回转身去
消失在密林深处

A Lizard in the Jungle

The tea tree stands cozily and lazily

With the mist

Its leaves from a big green palm

and press down to the earth

Withered leaves are sleeping soundly on the soil

I walk quietly

Alone and hurriedly

In panic, a little beast rushes away

A blue flame is evacuating from the withered yellow scenery

The missed child of the lightning

the mountain crosses through its abdomen

The flame that fell to earth is so colorful

That it comes out of a dream

burning and screaming at my feet

Panicking, its innocent eyes meet mine

purple jewels are thy eyes

With a frightened glance, a tiny tear I see

I mean to stare at it

But shaking off a straw and turning back with fright

It disappears into the deep forest

螃蟹的挽歌

湖水平,螃蟹生
耿直率性的黑脸汉
只因太过肥美
便被加上"横行"的恶名
五花大绑后
再也伸不出手脚
在滚烫的大蒸锅里
个个急得面红耳赤

哦,你也有受尽摧残的时刻
江湖里哪有永久的霸主
河之子
你怎么就认命了呢
在冰冷的盘中束手
在食客的嬉笑中粉身碎骨
大鳌也无法拯救你
涛声也不能将你唤醒

An Elegy for the Crab

Lake level, crabs born

The black-faced creatures are accused of their "rampage"

for their delicious flavor

Being tied

their hands and feet can no longer stretch out

In the hot steamer

all of them turn red with anxiety

Oh, you've had your share of brutalized moment

There is no permanent overlord in the world

Son of the river

how could you accept your fate

Stranded in the cold plate

shattered in the laughter of diners

the big claws cannot save you

nor can the sound of the waves awaken you

靠岸渔舟

银色的水与灰色的岸相依

水位被寒风刮得一天天下降

渔夫的蓑衣逐渐宽厚

蓬蒿在高处

思考着过冬的心事

水草在低处

少女般招摇

黑色的鸬鹚目光犀利

这一切都被阳光看在眼里

几位行人路过，驻足拍照

孩子们惊喜的欢呼

叫响现代文明中古老事物的意义

The Fishing Boat

The silver water and gray shore are intertwined
and the water level is blown down by the cold wind all day long
The fisherman's coir raincoat is gradually becoming wider and thicker
The wormwood is worrying about the coming winter in a high place
The water grass is waving like a girl in a low place
The black cormorant's gaze is sharp
All of these are seen by the sun
A few pedestrians pass by, stopping to take photos
The children are surprised and cheering, shouting the significance of ancient things in modern civilization

水 的 拥 抱

有谁被水拥抱过
她永远都那么温柔
冷静的爱
也会令人窒息

水从容地漫过呼救
直到淹没村庄的头顶
荷伪装成无辜的女子
夺我爱情,又粉饰太平

最好的伙伴被水抱走
童年跟着池塘一起干涸

The Hug of Water

Who has been hugged by the water
so gentle and calm
She always gives love like this
This, sometimes, suffocating will be

Calmly, the water overflows the cries for help
Calmly, it drowns the head of the village
Disguised as an innocent woman
the lotus steals my love and covers up the fact

My best friend has hugged away by the water
and the childhood dried up together with the pond

山　梯

站在一条铁链面前
孤零零地从天空垂下
它通往未知的地方
也因此具备了一些神秘
人们昂首云端肃穆
身后仍有更多慕名而来的游客
谁都不愿意当懦夫
只好夸大爬梯的难度
大肆渲染山巅毫无价值的荒凉
便于心安理得地止步

在险峻面前，才会了解信念的高贵
探索世界的先知所具备的勇气
像高山上的湖泊一样闪亮
向上，向上

周遭渐渐归于沉寂

天梯峻峭如严冬的静默

登顶后一如人们所猜

没有更为壮丽的风光

但我看到了

众多交织的目光

在脚下变得澄澈、艳羡和敬仰

The Ladder

Descending from the sky

an iron chain plays the role of a ladder

and leads to unknown places

thus possessing some mysteries

People hold their heads high to admire

Behind them, more tourists visit for its fame

No one wants to be a coward

thus they exaggerate the difficulty of climbing the ladder

and the desolation at the top

makes their cowardness reasonable

Only in the face of danger

the nobility of faith can be realized

The courage of ancestors who explore the world shines

like lakes on high mountains

Upward, upward

silence gradually occupies the world

The steep ladder is like the silence of winter

There is no more magnificent scenery on the top

as people may guess before their climbing

But in their intertwined eyes

I see admiration and worship

深　潭

向前延伸的荒凉
有着深不可测的幽静
冰凉的寒潭躲在这里

我穿过世间繁华而来
尽可能让目光柔和
生怕冷硬的眼神
会吓到这静谧之眼

这里没有树木
也没有一只虫子
四下搜寻，听到神秘巨兽的呼吸
虽然不见全貌，但我知道
脚下的土地
只是它身躯的一部分

潭水，是瞳孔里的秋波

我以卑微的身份，从这样特殊的视角

看到了大地之眸

对整个世界

充满了主人翁的一瞥

The Deep Pool

The desolation stretches ahead
with its unfathomable stillness
the cold pool hides here

I have come through the splendor of the world
to keep my eyes as soft as I can
lest the cold and harsh gaze
should frighten the eye of silence

There are no trees
nor a single bug either
Look around, the breath of the mysterious beast can be
heard
though the whole picture cannot be seen, I know
that the ground beneath my feet

is only a part of its body

Water in the pool, brightness in the eyes

Humbly and occasionally form this special viewpoint

I have seen eyes of the earth

to the whole world

gave a master's glance

一块化石

叫不上来名字的植物
早已在世上灭绝
在时间的挤压下
沐浴着今世温暖的阳光

高瘦的茎挺立着
像个俊美的王子
叶盘硕大,托着讲给石头的情话
昔时的邻居大多已不在
哪里还有人能懂你的心

活着只是一世
死去居然永恒
我们不过是陆地上的过客
你却知道海洋的诞生

立在博物馆的巨型展架上
我们观察、瞻仰
惭愧于人类的渺小与无知
那些属于宇宙文明的秘密
全都凝固在这时光的阴影里

A Fossil

Plants that cannot be named have long been extinct
They bath in the warm sunshine with the squeeze of time

Their tall and thin stems stand like a handsome prince
with a large leaf carrying the love words to the stone
Most of their neighbors in the past are gone
No one can understand the still heart

Life lasts only for a lifetime
but death lasts forever
We are just passersby on the land
but you know the birth of the ocean

On a huge exhibition rack in a museum

we observe and admire you

We are ashamed of humanity's insignificance and ignorance

All the secrets belonging to cosmic civilization

are frozen in the shadow of time

辑二　狂心若歇

Part 2
A Horse in the Prairie

在拉萨,仰望苍穹是幸福的

起伏连绵的群山托起缭绕的祥云
如同高擎着白色的思想
此时,大地静默
苦难的酒杯流出神性的酒
摔在地上一滴
碎成片片莲的花瓣

夜幕仿佛近在咫尺
星星缀在倒扣的黑色碗底
熠熠闪烁,眼波深邃而宁静
似乎在说,神灵触手可及

In Lhasa, Looking at the Sky is Happiness

The rolling mountains hold up the clouds

as if they were white thoughts

At this moment, the land is silent

The cup of suffering pours out divine wine

A drop falls on the ground

and breaks into petals of lotus

The night is close enough to be touched by hands

Stars are twinkling at the bottom of the upturned black bowl

with their deep and quiet eyes

as if to say that the gods are by our side

布达拉宫的傍晚

昏黄色的光芒漫过来
渐渐驱散一天的喧嚣
偶有阴霾,也被天空的手掌压低
像水流一样
淹没内心的焦躁
生活中刺耳的声音也变得柔和

天渐渐黑了
一个僧人斜着身子走过
他的后背被经文加持过
不畏天风的阴冷
似乎早已洞彻未来
月亮迟早会升起
公正普照大地

The Evening at Potala Palace

A faint yellow light pours in

dissipating the hustle and bustle of the day

some clouds are depressed by the palm of the sky sometimes

Like flowing water

The dust makes the piercing sound of life softer

and overwhelms the restlessness within

As the sky gradually darkens

a monk leans over his back

Blessed by scriptures

it is immune to the cold wind

and see into the future

Sooner or later

the moon would rise and shine justly and evenly on the earth

蓝色的湖

排排浪花被条条无形的绳索
束捆在一起
好像落入凡尘的孩子
肃穆而又恭谨
愿做今世修行的僧人
行进在追寻真理的道路上
为苍生的爱情洗濯身体

湛蓝的水,汪着一湖蓝墨的心事
温柔缓缓地流淌,容纳世间多少伤痛
我知道湖底来自天国的游鱼
溅起朵朵洁白的浪花
每一滴藏着尘世的悲悯

The Blue Lake

Rows of waves are bound together

by invisible ropes

Kids fallen into the mortal world seem to be

Solemn and respectful

I wish to be a monk in this life

marching on the path of seeking truth and washing the

love of the mortals

The deep blue lake contains whose thoughts

It flows gently and slowly, accommodating the pain and

sadness of the males and females

I know that the swimming fish at the bottom of the lake

come from heaven

They splash pure white waves

which contain the sorrow of the mortal world

夜宿草原

无比透亮深邃的星空
夜色的阴影如水宁静
躺在草原这张大床上
蒙古包显得多余
篝火的余烬渐熄
梦见你在宽阔的草地上
被月亮的火焰吞噬

血管里的酒精
随着白日的喧闹
在"丢失之夜"挥发
多么希望能听到一声狼嚎
触动骨子里的野性
让尖刀般的恐惧侵入胸膛
最好,让这草原之王

血红色舌头舔一下掌心
近距离感受粗粝的吻

我像孩子般陷入神秘的梦境
一条毛茸茸的大尾巴在怀中依偎
最后消失在涌起的雾中
这种幼稚痴迷的想法终止于
屋外一阵喜悦的欢呼
半睁开迷离的眼睛
第一缕清晨,此刻
正驻足在草尖晶莹的露珠上

A Night on the Prairie

With the incredibly bright and deep starry sky
shadow of the night clams like water
Lying peacefully on this large bed of grass
the Mongolian yurt appears redundant
The embers of the campfire gradually fade away
I dream of you being devoured
by the flames of the moon on the vast grassland

With the noise of the day
alcohol in the blood vessels
evaporates in the "lost night"
How I wish I could hear a wolf howl
which could touch the wildness in my bones
and let the dangerous fear invade my chest
It's best to let the blood-red tongue of the king

on the prairie lick my palm

then I can feel the roughness of a kiss closely

Like a child, I fall into a mysterious dream
A big furry tail nestles in my arms
and finally disappear into the rising mist
This childish obsession ends
in a joyful cheering outside
At this moment, through my blurred eyes
the first ray of morning is stopping in the glistening dewdrops
on the tip of the grass

草丛里一片羽毛

清晨蹚着河流般的阳光
草丛里发现一片羽毛
白色的,比天上的云还要细弱
我不知道,这是昨夜
哪位仙女幻化为鸟遗落的
我能想象上面未曾消散的舞姿
一颗美丽的露水睡眼惺忪
在上面滚来滚去
琥珀一样将晨光封锁于内

向着四下草原询问
每一棵草都在逃避我追捕的眼睛
虽是终无所见
谁又能否认青鸟美好的传说
在我深深的睡梦中到访了呢

羽毛啊,你太美
马头琴都无法描绘
不然,耳边怎么还会有沙沙的歌声
女神,如果你今晚再来
请一定到我的枕前
用你尖尖的喙
梳理我浓密的头发
敲击醉酒的睡眠

A Feather in the Grassland

With the flowing river of young rays

I find a feather in the grassland

It is white, weaker than some thin clouds

I know there must be a fairy

Who had fallen down as a bird

And the lingering dance can be imagined

A charming dewdrop is rolling

and rolling on it

Like an amber, the drop wraps the dawn in it

To the grassland I ask

Everyone of them is evading the pursuit of eyes

Nothing achieved

But who can deny that the legend of the blue bird had

visited my dream

Feather, you are so beautiful

that even a horsehead harp cannot describe it

Why else would there be a whispering song in my ear

If you come tonight

please be sure to come to my bed

and comb my thick hair with your pointed beak and tap

on my drunken sleeps

草原,也有陡峭的时刻

在敖敦塔拉草原
平地鼓出一块山包
不知名的绿树伸向山坳
远处白顶花边的敖包
像一个个硕大的蘑菇
夕阳的脚几度打战
仿佛一不小心就要滚下山去

小心翼翼前行
每一株草都不那么安分
只只纤纤素手
扯住我故作试探的裤脚
充满野性的伏石
一口咬住我的袍子
使我不敢轻举妄动

目光让辽阔大地变得苍白
浑浊的风声在狭窄的小路上呼啸
绿色的波涛让四肢无力
一次次拍打无情的嘲笑
索性变成草原的俘虏
顺从于神的默想
在露水落地的破碎声中
走向草原深处

Sharp Side of the Prairie

In Adontara prairie

A hill rises steeply

The unknown trees creep to the col

The white-topped oboes with colorful dress

looks like huge mushrooms

Feet of the sunset shiver

as if it was going to roll down the hill

With care I move on

But every grass is disturbing me

They grab my tentative trouser legs with hands

And a wild stone bite my robe

I dare not to move

The gaze turns the vast land pale

Sound of the wind howls on the narrow path

Green waves take the limbs' strength away

The merciless beatings are mockery

I give up and voluntarily become the captivity of the prairie

Obey God's meditation

And walk into the prairie's heart

amidst the shattered sound of dew falling to the ground

草原的性格

马蹄在安静的草原上爆炸
惊雷的回声在地面盘旋
征服由此扩散
命运已做好安排
纵使你百般柔软,也要去承受
冰冷残酷的践踏

时光恒久,任何人都会消失
草原哺育的牧民虽少
性格却如鹰如豹
毕竟幅员辽阔
多少不安分的心期待外面的世界
如不能像草一样覆盖大地
就是对光阴的虚度

绿色的头发里跃出敌意

排着璀璨阵列

成群结队如迅捷的狼群

直到一个叫成吉思汗的勇士为你洗头

将草原发丝拧成闪亮的箭

充满寒意,与敌人相争

Temper of the Prairie

Horseshoes explode on the quiet prairie

like thunders echo between the land and the sky

conquer is spreading

Destiny has been arranged

to withstand the cold and cruel trampling

though you are soft in every way

Time endures, but anyone will disappear

The prairie nurtures few herders

with the personality of eagles and leopards

Its vast territory also nurtures restless hearts

which are expecting the outside world

If footsteps cannot cover the earth like grass

it is time that will be wasted

Hostility leaped out of your green hair

forming a dazzling array

like a swift pack of wolves

A brave warrior named Genghis Khan washed your hair

and twisted them into shining bows and arrows

With their cold light, you compete with the enemies

傍　　晚

露水降临浸湿了双脚
那只金色的眼睛最后一次巡视
风吹来——
每一片草叶都载着夕阳
一片小小的、缤纷摇晃的光辉

粗粝的光
从穹顶沉甸甸压下
安详的海子折射那光晕
被捕获的蚂蚱
期待着发生"无罪释放"的奇迹

生活在城市的孤独深处
在这却又孤身一人
我在诗歌的草原诵读天空的句子

干净而纯粹的风吹过
绿浪翻滚,陌生而冷酷
为了在草上独善其身
只好继续逆流而上

At Sunset

Dewdrops wet the feet

and the golden eye makes its last routine inspection

When the wind blows—

every blade of grass carries the sunset

every small, colorful and swaying glow of the sinking sun

The rough light pushes its weight to the land

While the tranquil wetland reflects it back

The caught locust is waiting for the miracle of acquittal

Living in the deep heart of a lonely city

Here, I am also lonely

The words of sky I say in the grassland of poetry

Pure wind blows through the green waves

There is something unfamiliar and cold
To maintain personal integrity on the grass
I have to swim upstream on and on

退　　隐

寒气贸然袭击草原的客人
从毛孔掠夺酒精
帐篷后面的坡上
六匹骏马慢悠悠地吃草
眸子呈黑褐色
隐隐还有铁与火的痕迹
一切都是绿色：平展展的毛毯
身后的马蹄被风抚平

一望无际的绿布上
在稀疏点缀的鲜绿色草甸上
是花花绿绿的青年男女
奔跑、跳跃，比草间虫子还要活跃
朝着灰色树林走去
马鞍越来越远

幽暗、深邃、神秘而且操纵双腿
白色青蛙从脚下频频起跳
随着带路者的指引
庄严的大地开始撤退
湖泊向后移动
古老的故事
英雄的厮杀也在消隐
守着空空草原
牧鞭垂下

浓雾渐起,湖泊似乎高悬
草原几乎倾覆……又站稳了脚步
一次又一次扶着自己
在草尖上荡着秋千的草原
暮色中变得冷冽而自由
若你还不回到温暖的灯下
就要小心草丛里闪烁的蓝眼睛
草儿——这绿色让你颤抖
仿佛嬗变成火焰
它们伸出手去
等待善舞的姑娘骑马前来

Go into Seclusion

Cold air rashly attacks guests on the prairie

and plunders alcohol from their pores

On the slope behind the tent

six horses slowly graze

with dark brown eyes which are colored by faint traces

of iron and fire

Everything is green; hooves printed on the flat blanket

are smoothed by the wind

On the endless green cloth dotted sparsely with bright

green meadows

young men and women with colorful clothes jump and

run

They are more active than grass bugs

Heading towards the gray forest

saddles are getting farther and farther

dark, deep, mysterious and manipulative

White frogs frequently jump up

with the guidance of the leader

The dignified earth begins to retreat

and the lake moves backwards

The ancient story of brave heroes also disappears

On the empty prairie

the whip hangs down

As fog began to rise

the lake seems to overhang the prairie

The prairie is almost overturned...

Once again and another, it stands firmly

Swinging on the grass leaves

the prairie has become cold and free in the dusk

If you haven't returned to the warm light

the flickering blue eyes in the grass you should be careful

Grass—the green color makes you tremble

It seems to be transformed into flames

They stretch out their hands
waiting for the dancing girl to come on horseback

长　　调

美酒一开
羞怯便插上翅膀飞走
失去方向的俊鸟
拥着草原走进帐篷
长调里住着故事
绝非醉倒就能结束

爱情与友谊的隐喻
与梦境对峙
少女的舞姿
在目光的怀抱里绽放
北方之夜的寒气向四面
战略性撤退

此刻，我不再是我

变成寻找初恋的将军
诗歌与民谣胜利会师
悬荡的脚寻找流浪的村庄
谁不相信美人会回头
为了一句恰当的回应
端起酒杯
与两个逃逸的音符撞个满怀

Long Tunes

As soon as the wine is opened

shyness put on its wings and fly away

The handsome bird that has lost its direction

hugs the grassland and walks into the tent

Stories living in a long tune will never end even if they

are drunk

The metaphor of love and friendship

confronts the dream

The girl dances in the arms of eyes

The cold air in the northern night

strategically withdraw in all directions

Now, I am not me anymore

I am a general in search of the first love

Poetry and ballads meet triumphantly
dangling feet are searching for wandering villages
Who do not believe that beauties will turn back for an
appropriate response
Raising the glass
I come across two escaping notes

爱情的敖包

双手合十,默默念想

绕着敖包走了一圈

畅想着蒙古族青年幽会的场景

以罗帕相赠

用一粒石子祈福

让动情的草做证

托大雁捎寄觅伴的思念

虫鸣在夜晚变得温柔

落日在牧人眼里红亮

情歌也以流淌的旋律

织就溶溶月色

借着酒意

癫癫狂狂的遗憾

爱情虽美

可我没有长长的马鞭
朋友，请借出你的哈达
让我们共同
跳一曲草原凤舞

The Obo of Romance

Put palms together, I walk around the Obo[①]
imagining the scene of a Mongolian youth rendezvous
A handkerchief as the love token, they pray with a stone on the Obo
Grass move and wild geese carry the longing for the one far away
Chirping of insects is the lullaby of the night
Sunset becomes torches in the eyes of the shepherd
and the love melodies are woven with the flowing moonlight

Alcohol as the pretext, regretful I become
Love is something wonderful, but I do not have a long

[①] Heaps of stones used by the Mongolians and Tibetans as markings for roads or boundaries.

whip

My friend, please take out your hada①

Together, let's have a free dance on the grassland

---

① A piece of silk used as a greeting gift among the Zang and Mongol nationalities in China.

辽河公园

垂柳依依，秋风多情
满塘的荷被诗叫醒
平静如黎明的浮月
让人怀疑
这里是历史书上的大辽故土吗
还是说被勇士的马背
从诗意宋国驮过来
也许是英雄们厌倦了厮杀
筑起这滋养诗词文章的儒雅场所

穿过时间的屏风
一切缥缈如梦
所有的纷争已经在民族融合中
变得微不足道
片片莲花开放如美人

用澄澈的眼睛注视着当下的和平
翠绿的裙摆在诗人的抚摸下
愈加温婉多姿
只需伸出绅士的手发出邀请
就会纷纷上场
舞出
青翠的天真

Liaohe Park

The willows are weeping, the autumn wind is breezing

all the lotus in the pond is awakened by poetry

calm like the floating moon at dawn

It makes me wonder

if this is the spot of Liao in history books

Or is it brought here from the poetic Song Dynasty

by horses' back of a brave warrior

Perhaps it is built by the heroes who have got tired of fighting and longing for an elegant place to nourish poetry and articles

Through the screen of time

all become ethereal and dreamy

Disputes have become insignificant in the fusion of nations

Lotus blossoms bloom like beauties with clear eyes

gazing at the current peace

Their green skirts, with the touch of poets, become more pleasing

Just need a gentleman's inviting hands

they will all come out one after another

with their dance to tell the meaning of innocence

写给孝庄皇后

中午的阳光正烈
漫步到你的闺房前
面对谜一样的女人
我不敢以"诗人"身份自诩

你金色的微笑
缀着草原女性的刚强
英雄在你脚下抬不起头来
当忐忑不安追踪我的足迹
分明感受到豹子的威胁
我的灵魂在你面前
不过是微不足道的影子

你的歌声
在草原的血液上奔腾、跳跃

双腿在马背上有节奏地摆动
巫师的恫吓
八旗王爷的愤怒
都被你驯服
成为孤寂河上放逐的蓝月亮

我不愿意以这种境遇走近你
只希望见到你时
还是位多情的蒙古族姑娘
为我唱一曲充满草绿色气息的情歌
或者倾听比羽毛还要柔润的笑声
在星宿安静的夜色里
倚着云翳的山丘
在默默闪着光的敖包前
看一看又苦又甜的蛾眉

也许,你不做草原的公主
就不必去嫁给皇太极,再嫁多尔衮
做劳心劳神的皇后
如果做一个普通的平民
拥有朴素的爱情

生儿育女
用你深潭般漆黑的眸子
在迷人的霞光里
接受火焰般的赞美

To Empress Xiaozhuang

The noonday sun is shining brightly
Strolling in front of your boudoir
I dare not claim to be "a poet"
in front of a mysterious woman

Your golden smile
is adorned with the toughness of the women in the prairie
Heros at your feet are unable to lift their head
When my footsteps are followed by uneasiness
clearly, I feel the threat of the leopard
My soul is just an insignificant shadow in front of you

The sound of your song gallops on the prairie's blood
the movement of your legs on the horse is powerful rhythm
The threat of the sorcerers and the wrath of the Lords

have been tamed by you into the blue moon of exile on
the lonely river

I don't want to walk into you like this
I just hope that when I see you
you will still be a passionate Mongolian girl
singing a love song full of the sweet smell of grass for me
or listening to laughter that is even softer than feathers
In the quiet night
hills leaning against the clouds
are looking at the bitter and sweet eyebrows

Perhaps, you are not the princess of the prairie
you didn't need to marry Huang Taiji and then Dorgon①
becoming a painstaking queen
If you are an ordinary commoner
with simple love and values
praise like flames in the charming sunset
will fly to your deep, dark eyes

---

① Dorgon, the fourteenth son of Nurhaci, is an outstanding military strategist and politician in the early Qing Dynasty.

蒙古女子

以天地为舞台

奔腾的马背上翻滚着热血

太阳的独眼

盯着黝黑健硕的女子

她们蹚过光与影的河流

旗帜、弓箭……伴随着腾跃苏醒

堆积的黑云无声呐喊

萨满向长生天祷告

闪电如狼嚎直接

暴雨般的喝彩荡起一串回声

闪亮的战袍下丰满的身躯

令人心旌摇荡

冷峻的目光砸过来

积雨中的光辉远扬

雨洗过的马鬃
犹如方舟上的风帆飘摇
鼓响雨歇
嗒嗒嗒的蹄声从心上奔过

英姿从马上卸下
换下湿答答的衣裙
容纳夜晚的篝火
映亮粉色的花容
别人纷纷认领了属于自己的草原
我独追随温润的月光

The Mongolian Girls

With heaven and earth as the stage

the hot blood is rolled on the back of the galloping horse

They sun stares at the dark and strong women

Who waded through the rivers of light and shadow

Flags, bows and arrows...

accompanied by the silent cries of the black clouds

they are awakened

Shaman prayed to the Eternal Heaven

the lightning was like a wolf howling

and the cheering was like a rainstorm flashing with a

string of echoes

The plump body under the war robe

made the hearts shake

Their cold eyes hit the brilliance in the rain

The rain-washed horse's mane

was fluttering like the sails of the ark

Drums and the rain stopped

the clatter of the horses' hoofs were passing through my

heart

Their handsome figures were removed from the horses

And the wet clothes were changed

The night campfire illuminated their pink faces

Others have claimed their own grassland

I followed my soft moonlight alone

怪　柳

我知道植物会将根
深深扎进土里
却难以相信柳树将手臂
狠狠刺向天空
在科尔沁，我见证了
温柔的种族也有暴力
这里没有"袅袅城边柳"
也不似"枝上柳绵吹又少"
只有一股对抗命运的野蛮
这是战士与风沙互相钦佩的对决

我甚至觉得
这是走投无路的羊群
无奈被逼成雄狮
它们的愤懑和呐喊凝成一块块血痂

扭动的身躯含着对大自然的不满
像野兽一样
在这荒蛮之地不屈不挠地抗争
刺向辽阔的苍穹

The Unusual Willow Tree

Plants will root deeply into the soil

I know that

but I can't believe that willows will fiercely thrust their arms into the sky

In Horqin, I have witnessed the violence of a gentle race

There is no "Willows outside the city walls undulate in the breeze"

nor is it like "Most willow catkins have been blown away, alas!"

There is only a savage struggle against fate

which is a duel between warriors and sandstorms

I even feel that this is a story

in which a helpless flock of sheep were forced into lions

The anger and cries of willows are condensed into patches of blood scabs

Their twisted bodies are filled with dissatisfaction with the nature

Like wild beasts

they pierce branches into the vast sky

and fight tirelessly in this wilderness

风　沙

沙漠的粗硬的风
像铁一样轧平凌乱的脚印
在骆驼和骏马的领地
吹来一队辽金的勇武
望不到边的黄白呼啸
覆盖了天的影子

骚动的飞沙
占领每一寸裸露的毛孔
羸弱的睫毛蹙着无奈
定然也有难言之隐
南方潇洒的风姿
一朝晃荡成落魄的狂放

风沙如雷

将无法忍受的热情硬灌进嘴里
不能拒绝，也无法回避
让你费劲咀嚼
这难以下咽的诗句

Sand Blown by the Wind

The rough wind of the desert flattens messy footprints like iron
In the territory of camels and horses
a team of brave warriors of Liao and Jin dynasty is brought here by it
The yellow and the white whistle, covering the shadow of the sky

The turbulent flying sand occupies every inch of the exposed pores
The weak eyelashes furrow helplessly, there must be something indescribable
The unrestrained demeanor in the South sways into a desolating carnival

Sands blown by the wind, like thunders

pour the unbearable enthusiasm into your mouths

That cannot be refused or avoided

It is so difficult

to chew those hard verses

银　杏　树

伸手可触的黄昏
银杏树结满了白色的果子
摇晃着游子闪烁的记忆
晓月离屋顶渐近
天河也低低压在心头
我是谁？我要去哪里
疑惑的旅客在低语
九十年一结果的银杏都收获了
漂泊在外的人尚未扎下根须
金灿灿的落叶荡悠悠飘着
寻找着理想的落地位置
把一切都忘掉吧
但不要忘记少年出发时
心中那片芳春
野原上直逼人眼的葱绿

The Ginkgo Tree

In the twilight

the Ginkgo tree are covered with white fruits

swaying with wanders' memories

The moon is climbing up the roof

The milky way lowly flows on my heart

Who am I? Where am I going

The confused traveler whispers

Ginkgo trees bear fruit every ninety years

While the floating people have not yet took their roots

The golden fallen leaves sway and float

searchingforan ideal landing position

Let everything be forgotten

but don't forget the lush spring fields

in the young man's heart

when he sets out

芦花飞雪

在这秋高气爽的日子
我看到了雪
无数风中舞动的雪
没有让你感到寒冷
反而感到热烘烘、毛茸茸的雪

舟上轻歌荡着
那雪就纷纷起伏
它们聚集,又摇晃
像暗灰色的鼓动的帆
又像遥远古老的钟声

这时,你用目光吮吸沙土的香味
然后悄悄构思着
它们未说出的故事

每个路过的人都会老去
而它们年复一年重新生长
在遥不可及的思想边缘
如同智者，用毛孔里透出的
呼吸，呼唤永远陪伴的风
在季节的尽头默默零落

Reed Catkins

On this crisp autumn day

I see snowflakes

Which are dancing in the wind

They don't bring cold, but hot and hairy instead

With beautiful songs on the boat

The flakes are swaying with the notes

They gathered, swaying like dark gray fluttering sails

and ancient bells from distant centuries

At this moment, you suck in the fragrance of the sand

with your eyes

and quietly conceive their untold stories

Everyone passing by will grow old

and they will rebirth year after year

On the edge of unreachable thoughts

like the wise men, they will call for the wind that will

always accompany them

Silently, they scatter at the end of the season

广　　场

终于可以独享黑暗
旋转的世界已经停下
没有音乐,舞者失去了
火焰般的手臂
疲惫的草坪在沉睡
凌乱的脚印
被夜风吹走
迷茫的影子亦步亦趋
用沉默与我对话
黑色树枝在灯下轻轻驱赶着什么
广场从我前面走到后面
最后不知道走到哪里去了

The Public Square

Finally, I can enjoy the darkness
the rotating world has stopped
The dying music also bring away
dancers' firing arms
The tired lawn is sleeping
Messy footprints have been swept away by the night
wind
and my shadow has followed suit
confused in silence
The black branches are gently driving something under
the lamp away
the square walks from my front to back
to no where I could see

辑三　一念回心

Part 3
A Tree in the Temple

晨

想变成一个干净透明的清晨
候在你的睫毛上
只为你夜间苏醒
头脑一片空白时
第一时间受到你的垂青

Dawn

A clean and transparent dawn I want to be
waiting on your eyelashes
If you wake up at night
with a blank mind
I will be the first favored by you

暴　　雨

一场暴雨将我囚禁在车内
雨鞭抽打车窗
公路像小舟一样颠簸摇晃
夏天噼里啪啦说出一大堆话
窗外的世界仿佛要融化
体内也有一阵起义的句子
像是要破喉而出与风雨会师
一次又一次
压制要与惊雷比赛呐喊的冲动
井盖的嘴唇难以闭合
一声声呻吟在街上回荡
陷入困境的车犹如一座孤岛
与世隔绝，数着周围海洋的寂寞

A Rainstorm

A rainstorm imprisons me in the car

The rain whips the window

And the road shakes like a boat

Summer crackles with a lot of words

and the world outside seems to be melting

The rebellious sentences in me

are going to join forces with the wind and the rain

One, two, three and another

The impulse of yelling race with the thunder

is suppressed

With unclosed lips of the manhole covers

they groan and moan on the street

The car in this trouble is an island, isolated, counting

the loneliness of the ocean neighboring

叶片上山脉起伏

层峦叠嶂起伏的山脉
从一片叶面隆起
茎脉像弯弯曲曲的河流
牵挂着临河而居的河滩与院落

它在我的掌中静卧
叶脉与掌纹
犹如两条命运相交的江水
大自然从未疲惫
生命的启示藏在各个角落

Mountains on a Leaf

The undulating mountain ranges
rise from a leaf
The veins of the stems are winding rivers
nourishing the riverbanks and courtyards that live by
them

It lies still in my palm
With its veins and my palmprints
like two rivers intersect under the arrangement of fate
Nature never gets exhausted
the revelation of life hidden in every corner

在海滩想念远方

雪白的浪花被一缕阳光点燃
一望无际的思念熊熊燃烧
海贝上的清晨
被敏捷的螃蟹盗走
欢乐的海蜇一往情深

友人远远地呼唤
声音被海鸥啄走
汽车的轰鸣
吓退了拦路打劫的水禽

冲着大海咆哮
白色的火焰淬成蔚蓝
幼小的生灵泛着光芒
思念的人儿若在
大海该是多么欢喜

Missing on the Beach

The snow-white waves are ignited by a ray of sunlight
the yearning burns as far as the eyes can see
The morning on the seashells is stolen by the agile crabs
and the joyful jellyfish never stop giving love

The calling sound from afar of my friend
has been pecked by the seagulls
The roar of the car scared away the hijacking waterfowls

Roared towards the sea, the white flames are quenched
into blue
Small creatures shine with light
How happy the sea would be
if the missing person is here

视大海为新的目标

风撕开一切伪装
月光之手拉扯海浪之裙
谁都知道春天老了
仍在偷偷照顾世间的新娘

怀念神话时代的孩子
最终被铁铸的车轮碾压

悠长的歌声,乡土的叹息
森林焚烧后的疮痍不再重复
向往澎湃,涡轮制定好旗语
大海的骸骨上捕捞看不见的秘密

五指张开,明天向我奔来
五指聚拢,沙漠长出新绿

Sea as the New Goal

The wind tore open all the camouflage
the moonlight kneaded the skirt of the waves
Everyone knows that spring is old
but it still secretly giving its hue to brides in the world

Remembering the children of the mythological era
finally, they were crushed by the iron wheels of history

Long singing sounds and rural sighs
The scars left by the burned forest no longer repeat
Longing for turbulence
the turbine set the semaphore
On the bones of the sea, invisible secrets are caught

Opening my palms, the future runs to me
Fingers gathering together, green plants grow out in the desert

隐约长号

隐约长号响了
夜色中浓重的雾中
驶出思念轻舟

可以勇敢,可以雄壮
金属的喉咙莽撞如山雷
喊破满地滚动的石头

柔美的时候
并不意味着内敛和月亮
也不只代表妙龄女郎
听过如弓的长号
静静流淌,洗净森林
持续、有力、连绵不绝
树叶送来断断续续的抽泣

分明看见一把涕泪的钥匙
颤颤悠悠靠近一扇门
在都市的秋风中
迟迟没有打开

Faint Rings of the Trombone

The trombone rings faintly

In the thick night fog

the boat of yearn drive out

It could be brave or majestic

and the metal throat could be as bold as thunders

to break the stones rolling all over the ground

The softness of it not means introversion or the moon

Also, it not only means young girls

The sound of trombone flowing quietly like a bow

penetrating through the forest continuously

Intermittent sobs sent by leaves could be heard

I saw a tearful key is closing to a door trembling and

lingering

But the door had not yet been opened

in the autumn city breeze

凋谢之花

被雨水勾引,柔嫩的枝条上
一个个黄色的音符,探出脑袋

把梦境安顿好
就要找寻春天的初恋
那是一根根裙带吗
系在爱人的心上,直到四月来临

那满地金黄
不是霞一样的哭
是弥散了一季的
失望的鳞

The Weathered Flower

Seduced by the rain

yellow notes on the tender branches stick out their

heads

Put an end to their dreams

They eager to encounter the first love in spring

Are those girdles of skirts

Those tied to loved ones' hearts

until April arrives

The golden yellow on the ground is not tears like rosy

clouds

but scattered scales of disappointment

accumulated for the whole summer

黄昏截句

1

串串忧忧的音符
将那把栗色小提琴
听得
如泣如诉

2

一塘枯荷
把冥想的晨昏
刻成一幅铜版画

3

半枝残蓬
不愿入画
从匠人的刻刀下溜走
丛林自由摇曳

4

弯弯的石巷
把夕阳的思绪
铺成黛色的山路
一粒光滑的青石子
被忧伤击碎
被飞鸟衔去

5

涛声不倦的古峡
抱住一颗流浪的心
两间茅屋
徐徐从雨后长出

Sentences in the Dus

1

Strings of sad notes

make the chestnut violin

cry

2

A pond of withered lotus

carves the contemplative morning and evening into a

bronze engraving

3

A broken lotus
is unwilling to step into the painting
Escaping from the craftsman's knives
It sways in the jungle of lotus leaves

4

The winding stone alleys
turn the thoughts of the sunset into a bluish-black
mountain road
A smooth stone is shattered by sadness
and carried away by flying birds

5

The ancient gorge, with its endless waves
embraces a wandering heart
Two huts
slowly grow out of the rain

林子的悄悄话

1

不把它当作诗
离别后忆起的总是诗

2

早春的梦
溅起刺骨的泥水
泥泞路上
我们走来又走去

3

爱情无须表白

小鸟婉转的歌声

胜过千言万语

4

清晨之美

阳光斜去一角

展开一幅绝妙的油画

5

玉砌的林子

变幻着光色

沙沙唱个不停

绿荫小路

宛若一支透亮的洞箫

6

被阻隔的阳光

像被抓住的孩子

欲言又止,进退两难

7

唱歌追月
青蛙于沟汊唤醒芦苇
为月光伴奏

何必追风逐月
站在那里静静地欣赏

8

一位娇美的姑娘深陷沙滩
我与她相距不足百米
仿佛觉得离她很远很远

她婉转悠扬的歌声
影子一样跟着我
她款步走进椰林
倩影很快被海风淹没

9

在海滩捉到一只小螃蟹
金灿灿的螯比夕阳还亮
恍若南柯一梦
把它装进心里

回到酒店发现丢了
挂在云上的丝带
像个问号
黄昏里轻轻摇曳

10

疾风暴雨的夜晚
一次次被当作星空的叛徒
白天读不懂夜的黑
那时尚未有这支歌

11

小船装满山一样的青草
小狗像哨兵一样坐在船头
岸上，孩子们追着看热闹
吱吱呀呀划桨
岸边水湄的欢笑
把天上的云撩拨得通红
小船、小狗、小孩
逆光返入童话树林

12

不会没有悲剧
在只演悲剧的年代
一个女孩为了看场很远的电影
掉进一条小河
一瓣杜鹃苞苞
就这样随水漂走
那条小河
哭干了眼泪

Whispers of the Jungle

1

Don't take it as a poem

It always appears as a poem in old memory

2

Dreams in early spring

splatter with cold miriness

On the muddy road

we walk back and forth

3

Love needs no confession

The gentle singing of a bird

is better than tons of words

4

In a beautiful morning

the sunshine leaps off a corner

and paints a beautiful world

5

The jade forest is changing with light and color

rustling and singing sincerely

A song played by transparent flute is the green road

6

The separated sunshine
is like a child enchained
willing to speak but nothing heard

7

Singing in the moonlight
frogs wake up reeds in the shallow pond
to accompany the moonlight

There's no need to go far away
this show is also satisfactory

8

A fairymaiden is deeply immersed in the beach
Though less than a hundred meters
the distance is so far away

between me and her

Her gentle and melodious singing follows me like a shadow
She steps into the coconut forest
with the beautiful shadow drowned by the sea breeze

9

Catching a small crab on the beach, its golden claws shine brighter than the sunset
As if it is in a dream
I put it in my heart

Returning to the hotel, I found it lost
The ribbon hanging on the clouds
sways gently like a question mark in the dusk

10

Again and again

the night of the storm has been regarded as a traitor to the sky

The day could not understand the night this ballad hasn't been known at that time

11

The small boat is filled with green grass like mountains
and the little dog sits like a sentry on the bow
Children chased after
watching the paddles creak
The laughter of the water near the shore stirs the clouds
in the sky
The small boat, the little dog, and the child
All return to the fairy forest against the light

12

In an era where only tragedy is portrayed
a tragedy is so common
A girl was drowned in a small river

for the wish to watch a faraway movie

A rhododendron bud floated away like this

The river cried

till the tears dry

一个校园女孩

在雨后的校园里,她开出了一朵粉红的月季
纤细腰腹带着湿润的露珠
她的笑像徐徐微风
可以令任何一个醉酒的男人瞬间苏醒
有那么几秒钟,我萌生了采撷的欲望
我心里非常清楚
她,甚至所有来自雪域的女性
最能代表东方女性的美
一个回眸,一个撩发的动作
似乎超现实的镜头
她沉静、内敛,恰似春天的小兽
青衫覆盖下的刺朦朦胧胧地尖锐着
呼吸里有日落日升,像虚构的童话
唯有抑住心跳去阅读
才不会打扰渐行渐远的背影

A School Girl

On the campus after the rain

she bloomed a pink Chinese rose

the slender waist with dewdrops

Her smile is a gentle breeze

that could instantly awaken any drunken man

In a few seconds

I had the desire to pick the flower

but very well I know in my heart that

she, even all women from the snowy regions

is the best representative of the beauty of Chinese

women

Looking back or pulling her hair

all seem to be surreal

Calm and introverted, she's a small beast of the spring

Thorns covered under the clothes dimly piercing

With the sunset and sunrise in her breath

a fairy tale the scenery is

Only by holding heartbeats to read

will the receding figure not be disturbed

枯木龙吟[①]

杉，发出空灵之音

沿着千年历史

一次次被手指唤醒

这冰冷的丝弦

倾听生命的灵魂耳语

木头来自大地

被造物主临幸

让世人通过音符

回应自然的恩泽

时间带来了厚重

多少知音掩伏于纹理之中

阒寂中巨响

[①] 枯木龙吟，唐代名琴。近日在清华大学，我有幸一睹芳容，并聆听穿越历史的声音。

复归于沉寂
一切妄念化作尘土
琴有姓名
似佳人,似良友
弦声诉说寂寞
期待相思回应

我也因此,任由体内
尘封许久的某块魂魄
随着泪水
被这把钥匙释放
在那面文化的镜子里
世代目光如炬的文人脸庞
随一声残破的音节
被时光之河照耀

Dragon Chant in Withered Wood[①]

The qin made of cedar makes ethereal sounds

Along the thousands of years of history

It has been awakened

time and time again by the fingers

The cold strings

listen to the whispering of souls

Coming from the earth

and being fortunate enough to be seen by the Creator

the wood has let the world respond to the grace of nature

through its notes

Time brings heaviness

---

① Dragon Chant in Withered Wood, a famous qin in the Tang Dynasty. Recently in Tsinghua University, I had the opportunity to visit it and listen to its ethereal sounds.

How many bosom friends are hidden in its texture

In silence, a loud sound returns to silence

all delusions turn into dust

The qin has a name

like a beauty or a good friend

strings tells loneliness

wishing the lovesickness can be responded

As a result, I allow a part of my soul

that has been sealed in dust for a long time

to be released with tears

by this key

In the mirror of culture

The faces of literati who have been shining brightly for

generations

are illuminated by the time of river

with a broken syllable

清　醒

面包面对着火烤
终于明白
它再也不是
一枝沉思的麦穗

最先触地的雨水
打湿尘埃后
云朵成为深蓝的旧梦

破碎中涅槃
木头化作纸浆
青山不再是眷恋的故乡

归梦的残荷
破败中思索新生
留下最后一缕晚香

Sobriety

Facing the fire

the dough finally understands that

no longer a contemplative wheat ear it is

The raindrops that first touched the ground

dampened the dust

and the clouds became an old blue dream

Rebirth in the broken pieces

the wood turns into pulp

The green mountain is no longer its nostalgic hometown

Rebirth, the withered lotus are contemplating

leaving behind the last strand of pleasing fragrance

容　器

为了远离恶，涉过一条黑色河流
断绝滚滚红尘，以及所有的念想
如果写诗也是一种修行
日子也可以是一种容器
我就把自己装在一个修行的容器里
河流蜿蜒，犹如生活界碑，谁也不知道起止
在这容器的余生要时时警惕
防止涨潮的季节，让欲望淹没泥塑的信念

The Containers

In order to stay away from evil
I wade through a black river
stay away from the rolling world and clear away all my
thoughts
If writing poetry is also a kind of practice of Buddhism
then the days can also be containers
I shall put myself in the container of practice
The river meanders like a marker of life's boundary
and no one knows its departure and end
In this container
I should always be vigilant for the rest of my life
to prevent those desires drown out my belief made of
clay

山间诗心

雨水把秀草滋养渐肥
悄悄爬满古寺禅居
道旁繁花落尽
怀胎的果树为谁叹息
浮云满天,清风徐来
瓜熟蒂落的日子遥遥无期

高朋满座要我以诗招待
推敲词韵尚未成句
山上和尚解我心结
他一合十,山间一泓清潭
他一诵经,盛开满池红莲

诗心即佛心
欣然下山去

轻轻唱着浅歌
天上落了一幕清洗荷花透亮的细雨

The Poetic Heart

The rain nourishes the grass

and helps it crawl over the ancient temple quietly

Along the path

the flowers withered and trees have borne fruit are sighing

With floating clouds and gentle breeze

the days of blooming and ripening are far away

Distinguished friends asked me to entertain with poems

I refined the rhyme with scattered lines

The monk rearranged my thoughts

With his folded hands, there is a clear pond

When he chants scriptures, flowers of red lotus bloom

The poetic heart is also the Buddhist heart

Happily, I descend the mountain with a joyful song
A clean rain falls and purifies the lotus flowers

小鸟坐禅

傍晚时分
一只入定的小鸟
枯枝上安坐
如一团灰烬沉默
它用收紧的肢体语言
回应我好奇的询问
溪平如镜
像透明的翡翠
夕阳染红了水面
茶花的美目
被风撩得秋水盈盈

许是听够寺庙的禅机
小鸟与周身的一切
变成一句诗眼

山涧有足够的灵感任它挥霍
它却选择忘记自己
对抗身外的鲜活
这里似乎被遗忘
穿林而来
众水从石崖跳下
哗哗哗哗
一路跌跌撞撞滚入潭中

A Bird's Meditation

In the evening

a settled bird

sat silently on a dead branch

like a pile of ashes

It responded to my curious inquiry

with its tightened body

The river was as flat as a mirror

and a transparent emerald

Sunset dyed the water red

the beautiful eyes of camellias were blown to tears by

the autumn wind

Maybe heard enough of the Buddhist subtleties in the

temple

the bird and everything around

have turned into a poem

In the mountain stream

there are enough inspirations to let it squander

But it chooses to forget itself

and fight against the fresh lives outside

This place seems to have been forgotten

Coming through the forest

many waters jump off the cliff

clattering and tumbling all the way into the pool

鸟　　鸣

让鸟鸣唤醒树林
结出更多的鸟鸣
让诗句唤醒山谷溪水
记录神秘的幽静
让晨曦更像晨曦
露水清冽甘甜
蘑菇丰硕肥美
光阴从平面变成立体
多角度感受蓝天的羞涩

木屋湿润而祥和
阳光进进出出
不断加重着温暖的力度
石头似乎格外柔软
像生命一样真实

窗台上一声滴翠的叫声
教我学会爱上世间一切

The Song of Birds

Let the song of birds awaken the forest
and produce more songs
Let the poetry awaken the valleys and streams
to record the mysterious tranquility
Let the morning light purer
the dews sweeter
and the mushrooms abundant and plump
Time has changed from a flat surface to a three-dimensional one
feeling the shyness of the blue sky from multiple angles

Wet and peaceful is the wooden house
the sun comes in and out, giving heat to things around
The stone seems so soft that it is as real as a life
The song of birds on the windowsill
teaches me the great love for everything in the world

与石头交谈

平凡弱小的石头

睡在荒凉的坡上

等待一双温暖的足

也许看惯了无情的过客

故作高贵和冷漠

凄冷的月光不理你

热闹的树木忽视你

就连柔软的虫子也敢嘲笑你

把相思蹩在眉头

也没有遇到说爱你的人

若有温柔的目光掠过

不安分的心一阵狂跳

孤独寂寞的石头

你的寂寞与我一样

在这被人忘却的尘世

封闭幽暗的沮丧

学会了独自品味生活的色彩

不愿默默无闻化作尘土

坚硬的外表

将柔软的心封存于内

Talk to a Stone

Sleeping on a desolate slope

the stone is ordinary and weak

It is waiting for a pair of warm feet

Perhaps too many ruthless passersby

have shaped its fake nobility and indifference

The cold moonlight ignores you

Lushing trees are not your friends

Even the soft worms dare to mock you

You frown the lovesickness between your brows

but hadn't meet the person who says love to you

A gentle gaze will stir wild beats on the restless heart

Oh, the lonely stone

Your loneliness, like mine

has sealed the dark and gloomy depression in this forgotten world

You have learned to taste life alone

Unwilling to be unknown and turn into dust

your hard surface sealed the soft heart inside

审视自己

坐在草地上冥想
陷入空虚的漂浮中
我看到一个赤足的小人
干净纯洁的身体
蹚过汹涌的潮水
静下来，褪去衣服与容貌
静下来，褪去名利和欲望
像柔软的草地接纳星辰日月
在一朵花开放的细节中
剥开层层外壳
深入无穷的细微

我愿让自己
不断跳出自己
在空荡的宇宙中

感受呼吸的强劲
感受一团火的神圣
一束光的恒久
感受生命的核心本质
卑微与宽广的交替
粒子中的无限世界

Look inside

Sitting on the grass, meditating

I fall into an empty state

A barefooted little person

with a clean and pure body

is wading through the surging tide

Calm down, shedding off clothes and appearance

Calm down, shedding off fame, fortune and desire

Like the soft grassland embraces all the stars

and the details bloom in a flower

I have to open layers of shells and delve into infinite details in my mind

I am willing to jump out of myself

to feel the strong breathing in the empty universe

the holiness of a fire

the eternity of a beam of light

the essence of life

the alternation of lowliness and vastness

and an infinite world in the particles

这里静悄悄

请给我一个辽阔空虚的夜晚
装下所有的迷茫、委屈和不安
让一切繁杂的心事都静下来
梳理我敏感、沉默的神经
灵魂漂泊久了需要语言退让
当诗句无法表达内心
沉默即最好的表达
就像树叶纷纷落下而无声
无声胜有声
人潮涌动的时代
我是失去天空的鸟
唯有片片白云的愁绪
可以倾听我的诉说
在这个配合默契的日子
无数痛苦的眼睛睁着

躺累了就坐起来
在无声无息的枯坐中
对抗强大的清醒
我知道自己心有不甘
痛苦的来源是欲望大于实力
不敢抬头,害怕仰望的时候
到处是一片黑
也因此,在这样一个
空无一物的夜里
我仍然需要一点星光
点燃无边的孤独,照亮虚空
在词语的密密耕耘中
发出来自大地的颤音

A Quiet Moment

Please give me an empty night

which is empty enough to place all the confusion, grievances, and unease of me

Thereby let all the intervened thoughts calm down and my sensitive nerves be sorted

A long-wandered soul need no language

When poetry cannot express feelings in heart

silence can do it

Leaves falling silently

silence speaks louder than sound

In the era of surging crowds

I am a bird that has lost the sky

Only the melancholic clouds can listen to my telling

In this tacit understanding of the day

countless painful eyes lie open

They choose to sit when lying down makes them tired

They fight against strong soberness in silent sitting

I know that I am looking for more

the source of my pain roots in the imbalance of desire

and strength

I do not look up

for fear that it is dark everywhere

Therefore, in such an empty night

I still need some starlight

to light the boundless loneliness and illuminate the void

In the tillage of words

I hear the sound of the earth

穿过隧道

于困境中迎头凿开坦途
光明从身后落下帷幕
没有什么可以阻挡我们,哪怕大山也不行
隧道多么黑暗,多么阴凉
石多么坚硬,风多么迅疾

我在摆渡车上闭上眼睛
感受智慧灵巧的劳动者汗水的浓重
外面绿树茂盛,但它的深处
犹如体悟时间的艰辛,打开生活的钥匙
就这样默默地向着深处驶去

穿过隧道的一瞬间
真实的气息扑面而来
我看见一棵受苦的树

用密密麻麻扭曲的根，紧紧地抓着仅有的缝隙
好像随时可以把巨石的封锁撕开

Through the Tunnel

In the midst of difficulties

smooth path has been cut and paved

with light fell from behind

Nothing can stop us, even the mountains

The tunnel is so dark, so cool

The rocks are so hard and the wind is so fast

I closed my eyes on the shuttle bus

to feel the thickness of sweats of the intelligent workers

Outside, the green trees are lushing

but deep inside the tunnel

hardships of time and the key to life can be realized

Silently, the bus were driving towards the depth

The moment I passed out of the tunnel

the real breath rushed towards me

A suffering tree I saw

with twisted roots tightly grasping the only gap

At any time

the blockade of the giant rock could be torn by it

本书翻译：陈绍梅，山东人，翻译学硕士，现为国际当代华文诗歌研究会研究员。

Introduction: Chen Shaomei, born in Shandong, holds a Master's degree in Translation and Interpreting. She is currently a researcher at the International Contemporary Chinese Poetry Research Association.